More than Sisters

Susan A. Varnum

Harborside Publishing—Brooksville, ME
ISBN: 979-8-218-06446-4
Library of Congress Control Number: 2022916266
Title: *More than Sisters*
Author: Susan A. Varnum
Digital distribution | 2022
Paperback | 2022

This is a work of fiction. The characters, names, incidents, places, and dialogue are products of the author's imagination, and are not to be construed as real.

Dedication

For Albert, who encouraged me to be
more than I ever thought possible :)

Table of Content

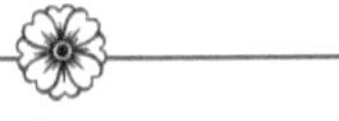

Prologue

This story takes place in Sedgwick, a little town on the coast of Maine. Rocky blueberry fields and woodlots supply a lot of the work for the native Mainers who live along with the lustrous Bagaduce River.

After the Revolutionary War, Township Number Four now known as Sedgwick grew in population and prosperity so much so that the Massachusetts Legislature incorporated Number Four as the Town of Sedgwick on January 13, 1789. Named to honor Robert Sedgwick, the English Major General who ousted the French from Pentagoet (Castine) in 1654, was the second town in Hancock County to be incorporated. Helen Gray and her family are based on the decedents of Joshua Gray who helped settle Township Number Four which is now Sedgwick.

Through discussions with my great aunt Ruth Gray Thompson, information from "Life and Times in a Coastal Village, Sedgwick Maine 1789-1989", information from "Descendents of Joshua Gray 2005", many google searches, and memories of stories told to me when I was young, Helen Gray and her family came to life. I do hope you enjoy your journey through a year in the life of a young family in rural Sedgwick, Maine in 1924-1925.

Chapter One
The Farm

Helen stood on the doorstep looking out across the frost-covered field. A heavy mist hung over the Bagaduce River where the summer-warmed water met the cool September air. On the riverbank fall had sprinkled its orange, reds and yellows among the evergreens.

"How could everything be so beautiful?" ten-year-old Helen thought as a tear rolled down her cheek. "How could life just go on?" The squeak of the hand pump from the kitchen brought Helen back to reality.

Helen Elizabeth Gray was supposed to be tending the chickens. She hurried through her chores. At the kitchen door, Helen quickly wiped some loose strands of brown hair from her face before she entered the kitchen. Perla, Helen's older sister, was taking the last pancake off the griddle. Helen washed her hands and set the table.

A heap of golden pancakes, crisp bacon and a dish of warm applesauce adorned the table. Large breakfasts meant long workdays. They were going to be harvesting the tomatoes from the garden today. Perla and Helen would be canning tomato sauces and pickling green tomatoes all week.

Helen sighed as she sat at the table. Nobody said much of anything. Pa and Jeffrey, Helen's 16-year-old brother, ate in silence. Perla was cross as usual.

Four-year-old Ruth, with her curly blond hair, didn't know who to go to for comfort. The family was just going through the motions of living. It had only been a week since Mama had died.

On September 17, 1924, Addy Louise Gray had died in childbirth. Then the next morning the new little baby died too. Mama was buried at Camp Stream Cemetery with her little baby in her arms.

Perla had to come home from Normal School in Castine where she was going to school to be a teacher. She was needed at home to help Pa with the children. Just like that life changed. Nothing would ever be the same again.

"When will Frank be picking up the creature?" Perla asked, after she dabbed her mouth with her napkin. Perla looked a lot like mama. She had the same sparkling blue eyes and the same pretty honey colored hair. The only difference was Perla always looked perfect not a single hair was out of place.

"Around noon," answered Pa.

Helen lowered her forkful of pancake dripping with syrup. She had forgotten that Billy, their two-year-old beef creature, would be going to slaughter this fall.

Frank W. Gray (Butcher Frank) owned a butcher shop in West Sedgwick, not far from Helen's home. He would be picking up Billy today.

"Pa, does Billy really have to go?" Helen asked as she stared at her plate.

"Helen, you have always known that he was going to be slaughtered," Pa said as he refilled his coffee cup.

Helen didn't say any more. It seemed like everything was dying. First Mama, then the new little baby and now Billy was going to slaughter. Helen wanted to scream. She wanted to lie on the floor and kick her feet and scream until the hurt went away.

"Helen! You're dripping syrup everywhere. Eat your breakfast," reprimanded Perla as she started to clear the table. "There is no time for daydreaming. We have a lot of work to do today."

Perla didn't understand. She was too busy being angry and bossy. When mama died, Perla had to give up her dream of become a teacher. This was all Perla ever really wanted to be. In Perla's eyes, to be a teacher, prim, proper, and strict, was to be a real lady.

Helen cleared her plate and headed out the kitchen door.

"Where are you going?" Perla snapped.

"To the outhouse, Perla or is that not allowed," Helen answered, her green eyes snapping with anger.

"Helen Elizabeth Gray, don't use that tone of voice with me," Perla said as Helen slammed the kitchen door.

Helen had no intention of going to the outhouse. She was going to save Billy. She had a plan. All she had to do was to get Billy to follow her to Mr. Rowen's apple orchard. Helen could hide him there. Then, she would have time to think of what to do next.

Helen gathered some carrots from the garden. She found Billy tethered in the barn. Luckily, Billy was really hungry. He had not been fed this morning. Butcher Frank didn't like slaughtering animals with full bellies. He said it made an awful mess when you cleaned their insides out. Holding the carrots out to him, Helen easily led Billy to the apple orchard. There she tied him to a tree. He would be happy there for quite a while. There were plenty of apples for him to eat on the ground.

Helen ran to the house, wiping her garden-soiled hands on her dress. She paused at the outhouse, straightened her hair and smoothed her dress. Then she walked slowly into the house. Helen went to the sink and started washing the breakfast dishes.

"You were quite a while in the outhouse, Helen," Perla said calmly as she swept the floor.

Turning around and looking Perla straight in the eye, Helen said, "I had cramps and needed to stay longer than I expected."

"What have you done to your dress?" demanded Perla, her face growing angrier by the minute.

"Oh, I fell when I jumped over the wagon tongue," Helen lied again as she wiped her wet hands on the front of her dirty dress.

"Helen, go change your dress, now! Ladies don't get dirty," Perla cried. "And you'll have to wash all those dishes again."

"I won't change my dress and I'm not going to wash those dishes again!" shouted Helen.

"Helen, go to your room!" demanded Perla.

"You're not my mother, Perla!" Helen shouted as she ran upstairs. "You're just plain mean!"

A few minutes later Pa came upstairs.

"Helen change your dress and come down stairs," Pa said quietly. "You need to help me lead Billy out of Mr. Rowen's apple orchard."

"Yes, Pa," Helen answered. She wanted to argue with Pa but she knew better. How had he known she had hidden Billy in the apple orchard? Helen wiped the tears from her cheeks and went down stairs.

With all the shouting, baby Ruth had started crying. Perla was rocking her and softly singing to her. "Just like mama," Helen thought angrily.

Helen walked past Perla without giving her so much as a glance. Outside Pa was waiting for Helen. Together they walked to where Helen had tied Billy. She untied the rope and handed it to Pa.

"No, Helen, you lead Billy to Butcher Frank's wagon," Pa said as he looked down at Helen.

Helen caught a small sniffle in her throat as a tear rolled down her cheek. It was a long walk back to the house where Butcher Frank sat waiting in his wagon.

"Helen, I know this is hard but it's the way life is on a farm," Pa said as he tied Billy to the back of Frank's wagon.

Pa looked at Helen with tears in his sad green eyes. Helen hugged him tight and Pa kissed her on top of the head.

"Perla knows she's not your mama, Helen," Pa said as he took Helen's face into his rough hands. "She's trying real hard to keep us all going. It was her mama that died too."

Helen looked up at him with tears streaming down her face. "I'll try real hard Pa to help Perla but please don't make me be a lady."

"Just do your best Helen, that's all I ask," Pa said with a weak smile as he ran his fingers through his graying black hair.

Chapter Two
Rabbit Ridge

At the end of October, Pa, Jeffrey, Uncle Charlie and his sons Moyle and Walter, headed to Rabbit Ridge to hunt. Two wagons were loaded with supplies and the next morning they would leave for a week at Rabbit Ridge. Helen wanted to go hunting with them. She wanted to learn to hunt. Jeffrey was so excited about going. It was all he had talked about for weeks. Helen wanted to feel the same excitement.

"Pa, I'd like to go to Rabbit Ridge with you tomorrow," Helen said as she placed a bowl of popcorn on the stand beside his chair.

Pa looked up from his reading, taking his pipe out of his mouth, "I see. Have you talked to Perla about this?"

"No, Pa, I thought I should talk to you," Helen said as she sat on the hassock at his feet.

Perla came into the sitting room with her knitting. She sat in Mama's chair next to Pa.

Helen scowled at Perla. She let her foot knock the leg of the stand next to Pa's chair. The stand tipped, toppling the bowl of popcorn onto the floor.

"Helen, be more careful," Perla reprimanded.

"I'll clean it up," Helen said as she bounded to the kitchen to get the broom.

Perla moved to another chair, while Helen swept up the popcorn. When she had finished Helen sat smugly in Mama's chair.

"Pa, do you think I can go?" Helen asked.

"Go where?" Perla inquired as her knitting needles clicked together.

"Helen wants to go to Rabbit Ridge," Pa said.

"Definitely not," Perla said sternly. "Women have no business going to a hunting camp."

Helen jumped to her feet, "Perla, I'm not a woman. I'm a girl who wants to learn to hunt and fish and take care of herself."

"Helen, sit down," Pa said calmly with a slight smile. "You're right. A girl should know how to take care of herself."

"Helen will never grow into a proper young lady if you keep giving into her boyish ways, Pa," Perla argued.

"Perla, I don't see any harm in Helen going to hunting camp just this once." Pa said, putting his pipe back into his mouth and picking up his book to read.

Perla angrily went back to her knitting. Helen kissed Pa on the cheek and hurried off to bed before he changed his mind.

In the morning, Perla woke Helen before daylight.

"Helen, there's been a light snow. The men want to leave soon," Perla whispered so not to wake baby Ruth.

Helen dressed quickly and went downstairs to warm herself by the fire.

Perla was putting some loaves of bread and a couple of pies into a basket. "Grab some biscuits, Helen," Perla ordered. "Pa's almost ready to leave."

Helen put on her coat and mittens. "I'll see you in a week, Perla," Helen said brightly as she picked up the basket and headed for the door.

"Be careful, Helen," Perla whispered.

"I will, Perla, I promise."

Outside the air was crisp. The boys were excited. The light snow was good for tracking and they wanted to get on their way.

Helen put the basket in the back of the wagon. Then she climbed in, settling herself for the trip.

"Girls at hunting camp are bad luck," Walter complained loudly as he elbowed Jeffrey in the ribs.

"I know," Jeffrey scowled. "That's what I told Pa."

The darkness concealed Helen's embarrassment. "Jeffrey doesn't want me to go," Helen thought. "He thinks I'll bring bad luck." Helen could have cried but she was determined to go to Rabbit Ridge.

"I will learn to hunt," Helen whispered to herself. "I'll show you Jeffrey Gray."

* * * * *

"We're here, Helen," Moyle said as he gave her a little shake.

"I must have fallen asleep," Helen chided herself.

"Would you like a hand down?" Moyle asked.

"I can do it myself," Helen replied sharper than she meant to.

Helen lugged her things and the basket into the cabin. As she lit a lamp, she could see a thick layer of dust covered the sparse furniture. Cobwebs hung from the rafters and windows. Helen found a broom and started dusting down the cobwebs.

"Just what we need," laughed Walter. "A woman's touch."

Helen turned to see Jeffrey, Walter and Moyle enter the cabin.

"Shouldn't we clean up a bit?" Helen asked.

"Sure, Helen. Let's clean up and waste a good tracking snow," Jeffrey sneered.

"Let her be, guys," Moyle said. "It's her first time."

"She shouldn't be here, Moyle!" shouted Jeffrey.

Helen sat down stiffly on a tree stump chair. She couldn't believe she had forgotten about the tracking snow.

"What's going on in here?" Pa asked as he and Uncle Charlie came into the cabin.

"Helen wants us to clean the cabin," Jeffrey answered with disgust.

"Jeffrey, you, Walter and Moyle better get started," Pa said. "The sun is coming up. Maybe one of you can get a buck in this fresh snow."

"Sam, I better go put the horses in the lean-to," Uncle Charlie offered.

After Uncle Charlie had left Pa sat down next to Helen.

"Sorry, Pa, I was just trying to help," Helen said as she sat her head in her hands.

"Well, Helen, the place could use some cleaning," Pa smiled. "You straighten up and I'll build a fire."

Helen took a broom and began wiping down the cobwebs and furniture. Pa put some coffee on to boil.

The early morning sun was shining through the windows.

"Looks right cozy in here," Uncle Charlie said as he came in from tending the horses. He and Pa then curtained off a corner of the room for Helen's privacy.

"Helen, Charlie and I would sure like some of that pie you brought," Pa said as he poured three hot cups of coffee.

"Shouldn't you and Uncle Charlie be hunting?" Helen asked as she cut three slices of apple pie.

"There's plenty of time to hunt," Pa replied.

"Yeah, this is a lot better," added Uncle Charlie. "The boys are always in such a hurry."

* * * * *

That afternoon Pa took Helen out for target practice. Pa loaded the gun and gave it to Helen.

"Put the butt of the gun up to your shoulder and aim for that rotten stump over there," Pa said as he helped Helen position the gun.

The gun was heavy and Helen couldn't seem to hold the barrel still. Helen took aim, closed her eyes and fired. She fell to the ground in a heap.

"Well, Helen, you just killed yourself a birch tree," Pa said with a smile.

"That gun's kinda heavy, Pa," Helen said as she rubbed her shoulder.

"Helen, I think you need to do some more growing before you can shoot straight," Pa laughed as he fired a shot hitting the rotten stump dead center. "Do you want to try again?"

"Maybe tomorrow, Pa," Helen replied. Helen hadn't realized how hard shooting a gun was going to be.

Pa and Helen returned to camp to find Jeffrey and Walter hooting and hollering. Moyle was hoisting a 6-point buck into a tree.

"Nice deer, Moyle," Pa said as he patted him on the back.

"Thanks, Uncle Sam," was all Moyle said as he went into the cabin.

"Never mind him, Unk," Walter beamed. "Moyle's always like that after he shoots a deer."

* * * * *

Early the next morning Pa and Helen set out to look for deer sign. The woods were peaceful and quiet. Helen's breath hung in the cold air. The smell of balsam, pine, and spruce tingled in her nose.

"Look Helen," Pa whispered as he pointed out a rubbing. A buck had been rubbing the bark off a tree with his horns. Fresh deer droppings were everywhere.

Pa held his finger to his lips. Helen stayed close behind Pa as quietly as she could.

"Helen," Pa whispered as he pointed out a large deer track. "He's a big one."

Helen could sense Pa's excitement. "Was it really that exciting to shoot a deer?" Helen wondered.

Helen and Pa walked to the edge of a knoll. Just below was a small clearing. The buck they had been following was drinking from a little brook. When the deer lifted his head, Helen heard Pa's breath catch. "What a beautiful deer," Helen thought.

The deer stood there proudly, his great rack of horns towering above his head. Water dripped from his muzzle as he looked in their direction. Pa took aim.

Helen held her breath. She could hear the bullet whiz through the air. Then there was a splatting thud. Helen thought she heard the deer cry out in pain. The deer went crashing through the woods. Then everything was silent.

"We'll give him a few more minutes," Pa said. "Then we'll look for him."

Pa and Helen walked a short distance in the direction the deer had run. The beautiful buck lay among some young pines. His side heaved as he struggled to breath.

"Helen, I have to put him out of his misery," Pa said as he loaded his gun.

Helen looked at the deer. His eyes were wide with fear.

Pa shot the deer in the head. The fear in the deer's eyes was gone. It stopped fighting death and lay motionless among the pines.

"Helen, do you know the way back to camp?" Pa asked.

Helen just stood there and stared at the deer.

"Helen!" Pa said sharply.

"Yes, Pa I do," Helen answered weakly.

"Clear your mind Helen," Pa said sternly. "Go back to camp and get Uncle Charlie."

Helen did as Pa said, not thinking of anything but getting back to camp.

Helen came out of the woods and saw Uncle Charlie sitting on a stump. He was puffing smoke rings with his pipe.

"Uncle Charlie, Pa has shot a deer over by the stream," Helen said woodenly.

"Helen, you go in the cabin. Moyle's got some coffee on," Uncle Charlie said as he pushed her in that direction.

* * * * *

Helen walked into the cabin and sat on a tree stump chair. She stared at the table covered with dirty dishes.

"Do you want a cup of coffee?" Moyle asked as he put a chunk of wood in the woodstove.

Helen didn't look at Moyle. She just shook her head.

"Why don't you and I clean this place up a bit," Moyle said as he started to clear the dirty dishes off the table.

Helen stood up and started to help. Moyle filled the sink with hot water from the woodstove. Helen washed the dishes in silence. Moyle wiped and put them away.

Helen swept the cabin floor while Moyle dumped the dirty dishwater outside. Moyle poured two mugs of coffee and set them on the table.

"Have a seat, Helen," Moyle said. "The place looks good enough for a hunting camp."

Helen sat at the table and took a sip of her coffee. "I don't like hunting, Moyle," Helen said in almost a whisper.

"I don't like hunting either, Helen," Moyle said with a sigh.

"But you always go," Helen said in disbelief.

13

"Yes, I always go and I always will," Moyle replied, "I have to help put meat up for the winter. I don't get a thrill out of it like Walter does. It's just something that has to be done."

Helen nodded her head.

"Why did you come hunting Helen? What did you expect it to be like?" Moyle asked. Moyle was seventeen-years-old but he always seemed so much older. He was like a wise old man in a young man's body.

"I wanted to feel the excitement. Jeffrey and Walter are always so excited," Helen said." I wanted to learn to hunt and take care of myself."

Moyle poured them some more coffee. "Do you want fresh deer liver for supper tonight?" Moyle asked.

Helen looked at him for a minute. "Yeah, I guess so," Helen replied with a puzzled look.

"Good, you haven't lost your taste for deer meat," Moyle smiled. "You know it's OK to be a girl."

"I know, Moyle," Helen sighed. "But I don't want to turn out like Perla."

There was a big commotion in the yard and Moyle stood up to go outside.

"You won't," Moyle said. "Because you're Helen." With that he went to help Pa hang up his deer. Pa had shot a huge ten-point buck. Jeffrey and Walter had also dragged a small spike horn into the yard. Walter wasn't happy with the small deer he had shot. He had wanted to shoot a buck with a large rack of horns. However, buck fever had gotten in the way of his judgment causing him to shot the first deer he saw.

Helen didn't go hunting again that season. For the rest of the week, she cooked and washed dishes for the menfolk.

Walter and Jeffrey didn't tease Helen about her not going hunting. They had gotten used to having a hot meal waiting for them.

Uncle Charlie downed an 8-point buck and Jeffrey brought in another 6-pointer. The week had gone well. Everyone was happy.

"Helen, are you coming hunting with us next year?" Uncle Charlie asked.

"I don't know, Uncle Charlie," Helen replied. "I think I need more target practice. I need to be able to hit what I'm aiming at."

"Yeah, Uncle Charlie," Jeffrey piped up. "I'm going to teach Helen to shoot straight by next season."

Helen stared at Jeffrey in disbelief. "I thought you said girls at hunting camp are bad luck."

"I'm sorry Helen," Jeffrey replied. "You didn't bring us bad luck. We each got a deer and I think you could get one next year with a little practice."

"Jeffrey, I don't know if I can kill," Helen whispered not wanting her brother to hear her.

"Helen, it's not easy to kill anything," Jeffrey said. "Just clear your head of that and remember how much you're helping put meat on the table."

"Jeffrey's right, Helen," Uncle Charlie said. "Will we see you next year at hunting camp?"

"I'll be there, Uncle Charlie," Helen said with a small smile. "And I'll bring a deer home next time.

Chapter Three
Perla's Thanksgiving

Thanksgiving had always been a joyous time when Mama was alive. Every year she laid out a wonderful feast. Helen dreaded the coming of Thanksgiving this year. Perla was making lists of what to cook and lists of chores for Helen and Jeffrey to do.

"Can we go to Uncle Charlie's for Thanksgiving?" Helen asked Pa as she put on her coat and mittens. She was going to the woodlot with Pa and Jeffrey.

"Certainly not," Perla intercepted. "I have a great feast planned for Thanksgiving. Turkey with chestnut stuffing, carrots with an orange glaze, cloverleaf rolls…"

"That's not what we usually have for Thanksgiving. What about suet pudding?" Helen said angrily.

"Well, I thought we'd have chocolate cake with cream cheese icing and a few pies." Perla said as she made more notes on her lists.

"Why can't we have what we usually have?" Helen said scowling again.

"Something different will be good for us, Helen," Pa said. "Go get in the wagon."

Helen could not believe her ears. Pa was taking Perla's side. "He was going to let Perla ruin

Thanksgiving," Helen thought as she stocked out of the house.

The team was hitched to the wagon, prancing and ready. Helen climbed into the back of the wagon and they were off to the woodlot to bring home the last of the firewood.

It was a rough ride. The once muddy ruts had frozen solid. Helen soon forgot about Perla's Thanksgiving plans. Her cheeks turned cherry red in the crisp cold air. Helen loved being outside. She wanted to do boy things, chop down trees, hunt, fish, just do what you wanted to.

"Helen, Jeffrey and I are going to split up the last of the firewood," Pa said as he took two axes from under the wagon seat. "Then we'll cut some brush to finish banking the house. You can explore a little but don't go too far."

Pa and Jeffrey went off to split the firewood when Helen spied the bucksaw under the wagon seat.

"If I cut down a few fir trees that should be enough boughs to finish banking the house," Helen thought as she grabbed the bucksaw and looked for a tree to cut down. "Getting the brush to go around the house to bank it against the cold would be a great help to Pa and Jeffrey."

Helen spied a fir tree with about an 8-inch trunk. "It's not too big," she thought. "I think I can cut that one down. It looks like there are some good boughs on it."

Helen held the bucksaw on one side with both hands. She put the blade next to the trunk of the tree. "The stump will be a little tall but Pa can shorten it later." Helen sawed and sawed on the tree. "This is hard work," She thought as she discarded her coat and mittens onto the ground. About half way through, the tree began to lean jamming the blade. Helen could not saw any further. She pulled and pushed on the saw for a while but it was no use. She could not budge it.

"Now what am I going to do?" Helen asked herself. Then she remembered a rope in the wagon. "If I loop the rope around the tree and pull, maybe I can pull it down," she thought as she ran to the wagon. It was not an easy job getting the rope looped up high enough around the tree. Holding both ends of the rope in her hands, Helen pulled with all her might. The tree cracked but not enough.

Helen tied the rope ends to the wagon and led the horses forward. The tree snapped off with a fierce crack. The bucksaw went flying through the air. The tree came down with such force it brought down the dead tree next to it. To Helen's horror both trees came down right across the wagon. Luckily Old Jake and Mary Lu, the workhorses, were used to hauling down trees. They did not run from the commotion. They just whinnied their disapproval at Helen, nudging her away.

"Helen, where are you!" yelled Pa as he and Jeffrey came running toward the wagon.

"I'm over here, Pa," Helen replied, she was still holding the horse's reins.

"Jeffrey, help me clear these trees off the wagon," Pa said as he looked at Helen.

Jeffrey and Pa cleared away the trees. Pa checked the wagon over for any damage.

"Well, the wagon's OK," Pa said.

"The bucksaw's a total loss," Jeffrey said as he handed the bent saw to Pa.

"Jeffrey why don't you take Helen home," Pa said. "Then come back and we'll finish up here."

"Pa, I don't want to go home," Helen cried as Pa walked back to finish splitting the firewood. Helen got in to the wagon with tears rolling down her face.

"What got into your head this time, Helen?" Jeffrey asked sharply.

"I just wanted to help," Helen replied in a whisper.

Jeffrey sat stone-faced for the rest of the ride home. Helen knew he was mad. Pa had just bought that bucksaw and Jeffrey had not had a chance to use it.

Jeffrey stopped in the yard just long enough to let Helen out. Then he headed back to the wood lot.

Helen walked slowly into the house. Perla was at the table going over her Thanksgiving lists.

"What are you doing back so early?" Perla asked with surprise.

"It's between Pa and me!" Helen replied as she stocked up the stairs.

Helen was surprised that Perla did not come upstairs to scold her. Actually, she was kind of sorry Perla didn't. Helen would have liked to shout at Perla. "It was Perla's fault anyway. She was making a mess of everything. Taking Mama's place. Ruining Thanksgiving. Why did Mama have to die?" Helen thought as she lay on her bed and cried herself to sleep.

* * * * *

19

Helen woke with a start. She could hear Pa and Perla talking downstairs.

"I bet they're figuring out what to do with me," Helen whispered to herself. "I guess I'd better go down and face the music."

Helen quietly walked down the stairs. She stood in the doorway to the kitchen.

"Perla, you need to be gentle," Pa said with a sigh.

"I know Pa," Perla said. "I'll do my best."

"Well, what's my punishment?" Helen said crossly as she stood with her arms folded and her face in a scowl.

"Calm down, Helen," Pa said. "We're not talking about your punishment."

"What do you mean, Pa?" Helen asked as she looked suspiciously at Perla.

"Well, Helen," Pa said. "Perla has planned a big Thanksgiving dinner and she needs your help putting it together."

Helen started to protest but Pa held up his hand to silence her.

"Perla has invited Charlie and his family to Thanksgiving dinner. Helen, she really needs your help," Pa said with pleading eyes.

Helen looked from Pa to Perla. She could not believe Perla would let her do anything but wash the dishes.

"I actually get to help?" Helen asked.

"Yes, Helen we'll split the menu," Perla said. "You will have a chance to make some fancy dishes by yourself."

"I guess I can help," Helen said suspiciously.

"Good," Pa said with a smile. "Helen, you stay home Wednesday from school to help Perla get ready." With that Pa went outside to help Jeffrey finish putting the brush around the house.

"Perla, is this a trick?" Helen asked.

"No, Helen, you really get to help," Perla reassured her. "Here's your half of the menu and the recipes to go with them. I've marked the ones you'll have to make Wednesday. The rest you'll make Thursday morning before dinner."

Helen looked over her recipes.

"Perla, are you sure Uncle Charlie and the boys are going to eat this stuff?" Helen asked. "They're used to having just plain pumpkin or mincemeat pie. Not mincemeat-pumpkin pie mixed together."

"Helen it will be fine. You'll see," Perla said with a smile.

Thanksgiving had always been a good time with plain food. Helen was not so sure about this fancy meal.

* * * * *

"Where's the cinnamon," demanded Perla as she scoured the cupboard for the missing spice.

"Right there next to your mixing bowl," Helen said calmly while rolling yet another dough ball for the cloverleaf rolls.

"Helen, make them all the same size," Perla criticized.

"I don't see why I just can't make regular rolls," mumbled Helen.

"What did you say?" Perla said as she stirred the gravy for the fifteenth time.

"Oh nothing, Perla, I'm just finishing up the rolls." Helen rolled the last piece of dough. She covered the pan with a cloth and set it near the woodstove. The heat from the stove would make the dough rise in no time.

Helen had to admit that Perla had set a beautiful table. The house looked beautiful, too. The fancy pies and cakes Perla and Helen had made the day before sat on the sideboard. The chocolate cake had sunk in the middle but you would never have known. The girls had piled extra cream cheese icing in that spot. The pickles and relishes were set out on the table in fancy crystal dishes. Helen never knew that Mama had such dishes.

"What time is it?" Perla asked as she stirred nutmeg into the squash she had just mashed.

"It's almost eleven," Helen said. "Why are you putting nutmeg in the squash, Perla?"

"It will enhance the flavor," replied Perla. "Helen, go mash the potatoes and stir in that garlic butter."

Helen made a face. She could not understand why the squash had to be enhanced. It tasted fine just the way it was. Helen was sure that Walter would have something to say about the bits of garlic in the mashed potatoes, too.

Helen helped Perla take the turkey out of the oven and set it on the cupboard. Then she slipped the cloverleaf rolls into bake.

"Helen, run upstairs and change your dress," Perla ordered. "When you come down the rolls should be done."

Helen looked at her dress. It had been covered with an apron all day and was not dirty.

"Do it, Helen, and quickly," Perla added.

Helen went upstairs and changed her dress. She hung the other back in the closet to wear another day. When she came downstairs the turkey was in the middle of the table.

"Helen, help me put the vegetables on the table," Perla said as she handed Helen the mashed potato. "Uncle Charlie and Aunt Samantha just drove up the drive."

Helen and Perla scurried about putting the remaining dishes on the table. The golden-brown turkey surrounded by garlic mashed potato, orange glazed carrots, nutmeg squash, turnip sprinkled with black pepper, sweet and sour pickles and three different kinds of relish were a pretty sight. Everything was ready.

"Helen, what's burning?" Perla asked just as Jeffrey, Moyle and Walter came into the room.

"The rolls!" Helen shouted as she ran and opened the oven. The rolls were black as coal. Helen slowly turned to look at Perla.

"Never mind," Perla said sharply. "Just slice some bread and set it on the table."

"Save those rolls, Helen. We can use them for target practice," Walter laughed.

"Walter, find a seat," Aunt Samantha said as she came through the door. "I brought some biscuits, Perla if you want to use them on your pretty table."

"That would be wonderful," Perla smiled. "Thank you, Aunt Samantha."

Pa came in with Uncle Charlie and everyone sat at the table. Aunt Samantha said grace. Then they all dug in. Perla had wanted things to be handed around the table in an orderly fashion.

"Oh, don't worry, Perla," Aunt Samantha said with a smile. "These men want to eat. It's a compliment to your cooking, the way they're digging in."

"What's on the carrots?" Moyle asked as he tasted them.

"It's an orange glaze." Perla answered. "I think it gives them a nice flavor, don't you?"

"Tastes good," Moyle answered as he covered them and everything else on his plate with gravy.

"Nice meal, Perla and Helen," Pa said. "Your team work paid off."

Everyone ate, talked and had a grand time. Helen was amazed that no one complained about the nutmeg in the squash or the pieces of garlic in the potatoes. Even dessert was a hit. All but a few crumbs of the mincemeat-pumpkin pie were gone. The chocolate cake was a little under done in the middle, but only one piece remained.

"What wonderful cooks you two are," Aunt Samantha praised. "I'll have to get some of these recipes."

Jeffrey and Moyle left the table to go outside. Walter wiped his plate clean with his biscuit and got up to leave. Helen met Walter at the door and handed him a brown paper sack.

"What's this?" he asked. "Leftovers?"

"It's rolls for target practice," Helen said with a smile.

"Why thanks," Walter laughed, taking the bag and going outside.

Helen put on her apron and started washing the dishes. "This is going to take all afternoon," she thought as she put some plates in the hot water.

"Helen, that's Jeffrey's job," said Perla as she poured herself another cup of coffee. "You and I have the afternoon off."

"What do you mean?" Helen asked with surprise.

"It's on my list. You and I do the cooking. Pa and Jeffrey do the cleanup," said Perla.

"Does Jeffrey know about this?" Helen asked not believing what she was hearing.

"They both agreed," Perla reassured her.

Helen watched out the kitchen window as Uncle Charlie and his family drove away in their wagon. Aunt Samantha was coming over the next afternoon to copy down some of Perla's recipes. She had really liked the carrots with the orange glaze and wanted to make them for Christmas dinner.

Pa and Jeffrey came into the kitchen and rolled up their sleeves.

"Ugh!" Jeffrey said. "I didn't think there were going to be so many dishes."

"A deal's, a deal," Pa said with a laugh. "Come on, boy. The sooner we start, the sooner we finish."

Helen walked into the sitting room and sat in Mama's chair. Thanksgiving had been a great time even without Mama. Helen wondered, how she could feel this way? How could she have had a great Thanksgiving without Mama?

"What's wrong, Helen?" Perla asked as she looked up from her reading.

"Everything was so great," Helen cried. "I even had a good time cooking with you. I forgot about Mama."

"Oh, Helen you didn't forget about Mama," Perla said sadly. "You just let yourself have a good time. We all did."

Helen thought about this for a while.

"Perla, do you think we'll ever get along every day?" Helen asked. "Do you think we'll ever be friends?"

"I think we'll be friends someday," Perla answered, "but we won't get along every day."

Helen sat back in the chair and smiled to herself. Perla's Thanksgiving had been fun after all.

Chapter Four
Christmas Knitting

Pa, Jeffrey, and Uncle Charlie had started trapping after Thanksgiving. Their usual catch consisted of raccoons, beaver, muskrats, mink, otter, fox, and the occasional skunk. Sometimes they even caught a bobcat. Their trap line had to be checked regularly, so each morning the men folk would load their sleds and pull them through the woods to the trap line. This year's early November snow made it easier to haul the gear laden sleds through the woods. The caught animals were skinned in the woods with only their hides brought back to the barn. Helen thought the heavy steel traps were a mean way to catch an animal. Sometimes an animal would chew its leg off to free itself from the steel trap.

Once home with the hides Pa and Jeffrey would put them fur side in on a stretcher so the hides could dry. Pa had made a lot of different size stretchers out of wood for different kinds of animals. The hides were put on stretchers to help them keep their shape while the hides dried. Once all the animal hides were on stretchers, they were hung from the barn rafters to dry.

At the end of each month the barn rafters would be filled with dried hides. This is when the White Free Company would come down from Bangor and pick up the hides. The man that came was always very happy, often telling Pa, "Sam, you boys have the best hides in the county."

One day after the man from the White Free Company had left with the hides Helen asked, "What do they do with all those skins, Pa?"

"They make hats and coats for fashionable people to buy," Pa answered as he stacked the stretchers in the corner of the barn.

"Gross, people actually wear dead animals," Helen scowled.

"Yes, Helen and the money helps get us through the winter," Pa replied. "Now get yourself inside. Perla will be wondering where you are."

Helen went into the house and helped Perla get supper. It was true Perla and Helen had gotten closer over Thanksgiving. However, Helen still had her doubts about Perla's motives. Christmas was just a few weeks away and Helen had to get started on some presents.

"Perla, do you think I could have some yarn and buttons to make Christmas presents?" Helen asked as she put a steaming hot dish for baked beans on the table.

"Sure, Helen, I think there's some leftover yarn in my basket by the chair," answered Perla. Helen went cold with anger. That was Mama's basket of yarn not Perla's!

Helen was quiet all thought supper. She couldn't let go of the anger she felt. While Helen washed the supper dishes Perla came over and began to dry them.

"Helen," Perla started cautiously. "Would you like me to teach you how to knit?"

Anger welled up inside of Helen. She couldn't believe what Perla was asking her. It wasn't Perla's job to teach Helen, it was Mama's. "No! Perla! I don't need your help!" Helen said loudly, her face red with anger.

Perla stepped back, tears forming in her eyes. Helen turned away. She wasn't sorry. She quickly finished the dishes and went upstairs to bed.

* * * * *

The next morning Helen climbed out of bed and sat in her chair by the window. "Christmas, what a wonderful time of year," Helen thought as she looked out across the field covered with sparkling new snow. A tear trickled down her cheek. All she could think of was Mama. Mama was going to teach Helen to knit mittens this winter. Mama had been gone for three months and Helen was beginning to forget what Mama looked like. Even in her dreams Mama's face was blurred.

Helen stiffened in her chair. A few more tears fell on the tangle of knitting in her lap. With the back of her hand Helen quickly wiped the tears away. "I'll teach myself to knit," Helen thought defiantly. "Damn, Mama! She left me all alone."

Helen stood up a little shocked at herself for having such a thought. "Sorry, Mama," she whispered as she looked out across the field.

Perla had offered to teach Helen to knit but Helen had said "No!" rather quick like and louder and meaner than she should have. But it was done, so

Helen would have to teach herself to knit. There was no way she could ever ask Perla for help now.

* * * * *

Things were tense between Helen and Perla almost more so than they had been before Thanksgiving. Perla didn't understand why Helen had become so nasty when she offered to teach her to knit. Perla hadn't told Pa about the set to and she couldn't bring herself to talk to Helen about it either. Perla wanted Helen to apologize and Helen wanted Perla to stop trying to be Mama. They were less than civilized to each other in the kitchen and both hoped that no one else would notice.

Helen often escaped to the barn to get away from Perla and one evening while she was hiding in the barn Pa was getting ready to skin a couple muskrat.

"I thought you skinned these in the woods?" Helen asked as she held one of the muskrats up by its skinny tail. It looked kinda like a big rat with an extra big leathery tail.

"I do but these got put in amongst the furs. Probably one of Jeffrey's jokes on Uncle Charlie," Pa said as he ran his fingers through his graying hair. "If I remember right Charlie was cussing a lot and looking for something just before we left the woods. You know how Uncle Charlie is always wanting to have the biggest lot of furs. Well, we were even today. These here probably would have put Charlie over the top. That is if Jeffrey hadn't of hid them on him." Pa laughed a little as he started sharpening the

30

skinning knife. "You wanna learn how to skin a muskrat?"

Helen looked at the dead muskrat, its eyes dark and lifeless. Could she cut the skin off the muskrat's body? "Sure," Helen said with determination as she reached for the skinning knife.

"Hold it a minute," Pa said. "Let me show you how to get it started and don't be so gung-ho about it. It's not an easy thing to do."

Pa pulled a chair over, "Helen, sit here and watch while I skin this one. Then I'll help you skin the other one."

Helen sat and watched as Pa held the rat by its hind foot and placed his foot on the rat's tail. He ran the skinning knife from the rat's foot to the middle of the side of its tail. He then grabbed the other hind leg and made the same cut. Pa lay down the skinning knife and using his fingers peeled the hide off around the rat's tail and back.

"Helen, always leave the hide attached to the rat's belly to keep the innards from popping out while you're skinning," Pa instructed Helen as he worked his fingers around each hind foot to the hide loose. Hooking his thumbs into the loose hide, Pa used both hands, pushed the rat's head into the hide and turned the rat inside out. Pa pulled each front foot loose from the hide. Then he carefully cut around the ears and eyes of the rat. Next cutting the cartilage in the nose pulling the hide loose from the head toward the rat's belly. Carefully skinning the hide from the rat's underside not spilling a drop of entrail. Pa then pulled the rat skin fur side in over a stretcher and hung it with the other hides in the barn rafters.

Helen took the other muskrat and Pa instructed her each step of the way as Helen proceeded to skin the rat.

When Helen had finished, the muskrat skin lay on the workbench. Pa smiled at Helen, "Good job little girl. You skinned this rat almost as good as Jeffery." Helen looked at the naked muskrat body lying on the barn floor in front of her. "Do you know how to knit, Pa?" Helen asked as she laid the skinning knife next to the muskrat skin on the workbench.

"I think you'd better find someone else to teach you how to do that. I don't think I could manage all those needles," Pa laughed as he put Helen's muskrat skin on a stretcher and hung it in the rafters. "Perla can teach you to knit," Pa said matter-of-factly. Helen looked at Pa with surprise. Did he know they weren't speaking to each other? Helen smiled weakly at Pa, "Thanks for the skinning lesson," she said as she left the barn and headed back to the house.

* * * * *

Helen looked at the tangled mess of yarn and knitting needles in the chair by the window in her room. She picked it up and shook her head, "I really need some help with this," she whispered to herself as she grabbed up the whole mess and went down stairs. Perla was in the sitting room knitting a pair of brown and gray gloves for one of the menfolk. "Perla! I need some help straightening out this mess," Helen said a little louder than she had planned as she handed Perla the tangled yarn and needles. At first Perla looked surprised, then her expression changed to anger but

32

before she spoke, she took a breath, calmed herself and slowly took the knitting from Helen. "I see." Perla said as she untangled the yarn from the needles being careful not to lose any of the stitches Helen had been working on. "It looks like you're making a scarf." Helen shook her head yes in response. "Stand behind me and watch carefully and I'll knit a couple of rows," Perla instructed. "This is how Mama taught me how to knit." Helen moved behind Perla and as she watched she remembered what Pa had told her, "Perla knows she's not your mama. She's just trying real hard to keep us all going."

Helen quickly learned how to knit and pearl. Perla showed her how to add stripes to the scarf and make a simple diamond pattern. When Pa came into the sitting room both girls were quietly chatting about their Christmas creations as he sat in his chair and lit his pipe.

"Helen, I'll write down the instructions on how to make mittens and you can try that when you finish the scarf," Perla said as she picked up baby Ruth from the floor to get her ready for bed. "Thanks, Perla," Helen replied as she looked up happily from her knitting. Perla softly sang a sweet lullaby to the baby as she took her up the stairs to bed.

Chapter Five
Christmas

Christmas was almost here and the barn rafters were full of fur pellets. It had snowed probably six inches and the temperature just hovered around 10 above zero. Perla had been knitting mittens for all the family since November. She had made trigger mittens, special mittens with a pointer finger and thumb so the men could have warm hands and still shoot their guns. Perla had made colorful mittens with patterns of snowflakes and diamonds for the young cousins in the family and gloves for the womenfolk. Helen had asked Perla for a pair of trigger mittens so when the weather broke Jeffrey and Pa could start teaching her to shoot a gun. She wanted to be ready when they went deer hunting at Rabbit Ridge next fall. Frowning Perla had said, "I thought you would want a nice pair of gloves like the other girls are wearing, Helen."

Pa looked at Helen than at Perla. Helen knew what Pa wanted her to say to Perla. So, Helen lowered her head looking at the floor so Perla wouldn't see the disappointment in her eyes and said, "That would be real nice Perla. I'm sure they will look real fashionable." Helen was sure she could learn to shoot with fashionable gloves as well as with trigger mittens.

For the rest of the evening Helen and little Ruth strung buttons on yarn making colorful necklaces and bracelets while Perla continued to knit. "Perla is almost as good a mitten maker as mama was but I'm not telling her," Helen thought to herself as she watched little Ruth examine a bright red button. Mama used to say that each button tells a story. Helen wonders what story mama would have had for the bright red button.

* * * * *

Christmas morning Helen is up early to put the Christmas presents she had made under the tree. She wonders if the presents she had stayed up nights making will be good enough. Helen looks around before she heads back upstairs to bed. Perla had out done herself trying to give the family a nice Christmas. The house smelled like gingerbread cookies and balsam fir. The Christmas tree in the sitting room was decorated with strings of popcorn and cranberries along with paper snowflakes. Helen smiled remembering making these decorations with Perla and watching little Ruth eat more popcorn than she put on the string. Helen heard Jeffrey stirring in his room getting ready to go out and tend the animals and hurried to her room.

* * * * *

Helen woke to a wonderful smell. Cinnamon rolls? Perla had made cinnamon rolls for Christmas breakfast, just like mama. Helen felt the anger grow inside her, then she remembered what Pa had said, "Perla knows she's not your mama. She's just trying real hard to keep us all going." Helen took a couple deep breaths and looked out the window at the crusty snow. "Mama help me understand Perla," Helen whispered as a tear rolled down her cheek.

"Helen, time for Christmas breakfast," Pa said as he knocked on the door.

"Coming Pa!" Helen answered as she quickly washed her face in her wash basin.

Everyone was waiting at the table when Helen came down. A platter of hot cinnamon rolls sat in the middle of the table. They looked quite a bit browner than mama's cinnamon rolls which made Helen smile.

"Helen can you please sit down? The smell of these cinnamon rolls is driving me crazy," Jeffrey demanded. Pa loudly cleared his throat. "Oh, aw, Merry Christmas Helen, will you please take a seat?" Jeffrey said sweetly as Helen sat down at the table.

"Merry Christmas to you to Jeffrey," Helen said as she smiled at Jeffrey.

"Join hands," Pa said quietly and everyone even little Ruth did what Pa had said and Pa began. "Thank you, Lord, for this wonderful breakfast Perla has prepared on Jesus's birthday, Amen."

"Happy Birthday, Jesus!" little Ruth cheered and clapped her hands.

Everyone laughed as the cinnamon rolls were passed around the table.

* * * * *

At the Christmas tree Helen read the names on the presents to little Ruth before she handed out a present. Jeffrey and Pa were pleased with the handsome red and orange scarves Helen had knit for them. Perla immediately put on her cream-colored scarf telling Helen, "This is a very fashionable scarf. It will go with all my outfits."

Little Ruth tied her scarf around her head saying, "Keep my ears warm." And everyone laughed.

Helen thanked Perla for the handsome gloves, giving her a hug.

"Helen," Perla said. "Look again under the tree. I believe there is another present there for you from me." Helen looked under the tree again and there hung a pair of trigger mittens with Helen's name on them.

"This way Helen, you can have a fashionable pair and a hunting pair," Perla said with a smile. Helen hugged Perla again this time telling Perla, "I love you, Perla. Thank you." Both girls cried and hugged again.

Pa had a fox stole made for Perla and she told him, "Pa these are all the rage in New York." As she kissed him on the cheek.

"Perla, you can wear it to the New Year's Eve dance next week," Pa said with a smile. Perla blushed wondering how Pa knew the new Baptist minister had asked her to the dance.

"Perla, Perla!" shouted little Ruth. "Look what me got!" Little Ruth ran to Perla with a soft white rabbit skin cape with a hood.

"Oh, Ruth," Perla exclaimed. "Try it on." Perla put the cape on Ruth tying the soft leather laces with the puffy rabbit fur puffs at the ends in a loose bow at her neck. Little Ruth twirled around the room laughing as she danced.

While everyone was watching little Ruth twirl, Pa slipped out to the shed to bring in Jeffrey and Helen's presents. When he came back into the sitting room, he was carrying two Cape Racers and said, "These were too big to put under the tree."

Ruth stopped dancing and clapped her hands. Helen and Jeffrey stood up and just looked at Pa. They had never dreamed that they would have Cape Racers the fastest sleds ever on crusty snow.

"Oh, Pa! Thank you!" they both shouted as they ran and hugged their father.

* * * * *

Now Cape Racers are a special type of hand sled that were invented in Cape Rosier. A small community in Brooksville about as close to the Atlantic Ocean as you can get. In the winter sledding was a great sport for adults as well as youngsters. In the fall Thurston's Meadow, out by Old County Road, was always flooded. When it froze solid in the winter it was a great place for sliding and skating. Cape Racing could be very competitive especially when there was a good crust on the snow and this winter, 1924-1925 was no exception. The crust on the snow was thick and at places like Thurston's Meadow you could go over a half mile in a single slide.

Jeffrey was thinking this very thing as he waxed the runners of his new sled. "Pa, can we go to Thurston's Meadow tomorrow?" Jeffrey asked as he ran the cake of paraffin wax up and down the runner of his new sled.

"After chores, tomorrow we'll go, build a bonfire, and sled for the day," Pa answered. "Uncle Charlie and his family will be there, too."

"Great!" shouted Jeffrey. "Me, Walter, and Moyle can race. See who can go faster and farther."

"Walter, Moyle, and I," corrected Perla, who had been sitting quietly by the sitting room stove crocheting a lace doily. Jeffrey smiled at Perla and stuck out his tongue. Pa gave Jeffrey a stern look.

"She's my sister, not my mother," Jeffrey said his face turning red as he continued to wax the sled runners. "Sorry, Perla," he muttered softly.

Helen had been quietly listening to the conversation as she waxed the runners on her sled. She was surprised at what Jeffrey had said about Perla. Did he too feel that Perla as trying to be mama? Helen decided not to say anything, Perla looked surprised and hurt enough, she didn't need to make it worse.

"Pa what if I pack a picnic lunch of turkey sandwiches, cookies, hot chocolate. Christmas leftovers, make a sledding party out of it," Perla said as she continued to crochet the doily stopping only to look up at Pa for his response.

"That sounds great," Pa said. "We'll make a day of it."

* * * * *

After chores the menfolk, Pa, Uncle Charlie, Jeffrey, Moyle, and Walter took a load of wood to Thurston's

Meadow to get the bonfire ready. Aunt Samantha was in the kitchen with Perla making sandwiches and packing the picnic. Helen was in charge of getting little Ruth ready, dressed warm enough to be outside in the cold all day.

"String buttons," Ruth said as she dumped the container of buttons all over the sitting room floor.

"Ruth, we need to pick these up," Helen said with a smile. "We need to get ready to go to a picnic and bonfire."

"Fun!" Little Ruth shouted as she ran to get her coat and boots.

"No, no Ruth we need to pick up the buttons first," Helen said as she tried to herd little Ruth back into the sitting room.

"You pickup, me go picnic," Ruth quarreled as she struggled to put on her boots and coat.

Helen took the coat and boots away from Ruth, "I'll help you pick up the buttons first, then I'll help you put on your coat," Helen coaxed as sweetly as she could.

Little Ruth began to scream, "Go picnic! No buttons!" Bringing Perla into the sitting room.

"What is going on!" Perla demanded as she scanned the sitting room. "Helen, pick up these buttons and I'll get Ruth dressed."

"No! Perla!" shouted Helen. "If you want to be our mother, you should make little Ruth pick up after herself. She made the mess!" And with that said Helen stomped upstairs.

A few minutes later Aunt Samantha knocked on Helen's door. "May I come in dear?" she quietly asked.

Helen opened the door and let Aunt Samantha into the room, walked over and sat on her bed and starred out the window. Aunt Samantha sat down next to Helen on the bed.

"Helen," Aunt Samantha said quietly. "Perla is not trying to be your mother."

"Yes, she is!" Helen said sharper than she meant too. "Sorry, Aunt Samantha, but everything Perla does is almost exactly the way mama did it."

"Well, Perla lived with your mama for 18 years. She watched everything your mama did. She is trying to fill your mama's shoes. Perla is trying to be more than a sister, she's trying to make sure you, Jeffrey, and little Ruth are raised the way your mama would have wanted you raised. Perla doesn't want to be your mama but she does want your mama to be proud of all of you," Aunt Samantha said as she wrapped Helen in a warm hug.

"Why did mama have to die, Aunt Samantha? I miss her so," Helen cried into Aunt Samantha's shoulder.

"I don't know, child," responded Aunt Samantha. "Just know that your mama is watching from Heaven and probably praying for you girls to get along." Helen let go of Aunt Samantha and looked down at the floor. A tear slid down her face, dropped to the floor, splashing on the hardwood.

"Helen, wash and dry your face. Get your things on and be down stairs in five minutes," Aunt Samantha quietly demanded as she slipped out of the room and closed the door.

Helen stood woodenly by the wash basin, washed and dried her face. Put on her outside winter clothes and picked up the trigger mittens Perla had made for her. Made special for her. Yes, Perla was trying to be more than a sister. She was trying to be Helen's friend. A bossy friend Helen had to admit but Perla was trying. Then Helen thought to herself. "Am I trying?" Helen knew the answer was no, she wasn't trying. She was still mad that mama had died and was taking it out on Perla. That was the truth of it. Now Helen had to do her best to be more than a sister. Helen slipped on the trigger mittens and went downstairs to join the others.

* * * * *

The bonfire was blazing when they reached Thurston's Meadow. Moyle was checking the thickness of the crust on the snow, while Walter and Jeffrey put more wood on the bonfire. Jeffrey smiled when he saw Pa drive up with the girls in the wagon.

"Now we can start the race!" shouted Jeffrey. "You ready to lose Walter."

"In your dreams," laughed Walter.

"What's the plan?" asked Moyle. "Are we racing all at once or individually and compare how far each of us goes?"

"I think individually is the safest," replied Pa.

"Yes," agreed Uncle Charlie. "Remember the crash that happened last year. Thomas Carter and Lee Black were racing down this very hill and crashed. Thomas ended up with a broken arm and Lee had a concussion. So individually is the only way."

With the flip of a coin, it was decided that Walter would go first, then Jeff, and last Moyle. The one who slid the farthest would be awarded the title of King of Thurston's Meadow. Helen thought this was great fun but she definitely didn't want to be in the race. Not this year anyway. She needed to practice with her new Cape Racer. Learn how to make the sled go where she wanted it to go.

Walter was at the top of the hill readying himself for the slide down the hill. His mother, Aunt Samantha was holding tight to Uncle Charlie. She was worried one of the boys might get hurt as the cascaded down the hill.

"Sam the boys will be fine. Don't worry," Charlie said as he squeezed Aunt Samantha in a tight reassuring hug.

Walter let out a loud whoop as he ran and jumped onto his sled flying faster than fast down the crusted hill and down through the meadow. He made it just to the half mile mark when the sled hit a small tree stump sticking up through the snow. The sled stopped abruptly sending Walter skittering across the icy snow crust another 100 feet. Walter jumped up, let out another loud whoop and danced a little jig. He grabbed his sled and slip walked across the meadow.

"Beat that, Jeffrey," boasted Walter. "That was an easy half mile plus. My skidding another 100 feet should count too."

Jeffrey rolled his eyes at Walter. Helen could tell Jeffrey was nervous. She didn't know if it was because Jeffrey was worried he wouldn't make it to the half mile mark or the teasing he would get from Walter if he didn't make it. Helen gave Jeffrey a thumbs up so he would know she was rooting for him.

At the top of the hill Jeffrey readied himself. He looked down the hill, walked back a couple yards, and then with all his might ran and jumped onto his sled. Lickity-split Jeffrey went sailing down the hill. Helen heard Pa suck in his breath and Perla gasp, clasping her hand to her mouth. Helen was not worried she knew her brother was strong and could maneuver his sled. Jeffrey was sure going fast enough to make it past the half mile marker.

Jeffrey sailed past the half mile mark swerving around the small tree stump that had sent Walter flying. About half way across the frozen meadow still sliding along at a good clip, Jeffrey rolled off his sled. Just like that Jeffrey had stopped sledding. Helen was dumb founded she didn't know what to think. Why had Jeffrey just rolled off his sled, he could have slid on for a long way?

Pa was laughing and Perla was clapping hands as Jeffrey walked up to them.

"Nice sledding, Jeff," Pa said as he patted Jeffrey on the back.

"Why did you roll of your sled?" Helen demanded. "You could have slid on a lot further."

"Let's watch Moyle to see how he does," Jeffrey said as he turned to watch Moyle take his turn sledding. And that was all Jeffrey said about it. He didn't answer Helen's question and no one else asked him about it either.

Moyle was at the top of the hill, his sled placed just where he wanted it. Helen knew Moyle wouldn't let out a whoop like Walter did, Moyle was always quiet and reserved. Moyle walked back a couple yards just like Jeffrey did, then ran full speed and jumped onto his sled. Hurtling down the hill at top speed, Moyle soared past the half mile mark. Then about half way across the meadow Moyle rolled off his sled at almost the exact spot Jeffrey did. Helen's mouth dropped open and she heard Pa say, "Well, I'll be."

"Something's up," Helen thought to herself, "The boys had planned this, she knew it. But there was no use asking they surely wouldn't tell her."

"Well, I guess there are two Kings of Thurston's Meadow this year!" shouted Uncle Charlie. "Moyle and Jeffrey!"

"Let's have some lunch," Pa said. "Then we all can sled on the other side of the hill. Not so steep on that side."

Everyone filled their stomachs with turkey sandwiches slathered with cranberry sauce, loads of cookies, and hot chocolate. Pa took little Ruth down the hill on his sled, Ruth laughing with delight all the way. When Pa offered Perla a ride, she declined saying Aunt Samantha needed her help packing up the leftovers from the picnic lunch. Helen went down many times on her new Cape Racer ending in a heap at the bottom of the hill a couple times. Moyle and Jeffrey gave her pointers on how to use her body to maneuver the sled. Soon Helen was handling the sled almost as good as Jeffrey and Moyle. Well, almost. With a lot more practice Helen figured she might be able to enter the King of Thurston's Meadow race next year.

Chapter Six
The Smelt Tent

The farm was all buttoned up for winter and the last of the firewood was stacked. The Bagaduce River had frozen over so Pa and Jeffrey started preparing their gear for winter fishing. It had been decided the week before that another smelt tent would be built for Jeffrey to use. Helen really wanted to help build the smelt tent. So, after school she crept up to the barn to watch Jeffrey and Pa work.

When Helen reached the barn, she went in through the side door so she wouldn't be seen. She hid behind some hay bales to watch Pa and Jeffrey. They were talking about the eels they had caught that day on the river. Pa and Jeffrey had built a wooden frame six feet long by four feet wide. It looked just like a tiny house, only there was a rectangular hole at one end of the floor. Jeffery was covering the tiny house frame with unbleached muslin nailing it tight over a wooden frame. A small door had been placed on one side of the smelt tent. Helen watched Pa with fascination as he made a woodstove out of a metal five-gallon oil can on his workbench. It would be used to heat the tent while Jeffrey fished.

Once Jeffrey finished covering the smelt tent with muslin he went and found some old gray paint. When he opened the can he used a wooden lath to stir the oil back into the paint solids. Painting the tent would make it weather tight keeping out the wind and rain.

"Pa, I think I'll paint my tent after supper," Jeffrey told Pa as he carefully tapped the old paint can cover back into place.

"Fine, son," Pa replied as he put the little stove into the tent, securing the stove pipe to the stove and through its opening in the tent roof. "Let's finish up the barn chores before going in, Jeff. You should be able to have your tent finished up before bed tonight. Then we can haul it to the river tomorrow."

Helen suddenly realized she should be inside helping with supper. She hurried back to the house, the kitchen door slamming behind her.

"Where have you been, Helen," Perla asked as she slipped a pan of biscuits in the oven.

"I had to go to the outhouse," Helen lied as she hurried upstairs to change out of my school clothes.

When she returned to the kitchen, she could see they were having baked eels and hot biscuits for supper. Eels look like snakes with fins. They may be nasty looking alive but they sure tasted good. Perla had rolled the skinned eel in a mixture of flour, salt and pepper. Frying them in hot pork fat drippings until each piece was golden brown. After the eel was nicely brown Perla put the cover on the spider (a frying pan with legs). Then put it in the oven so the eel would finish cooking.

Helen hurried and set the table. Perla took the eels and biscuits from the oven putting them on platters.

Pa and Jeffrey came into the kitchen from the barn having finished the evening chores and washed up at the sink. Pa picked baby Ruth up from the floor tossing her into the air. Ruth squealed with delight.

"Pa, don't get her all riled up before supper," Perla laughed as she put a dish of molasses on the table.

"It's good for her digestion if she's going to eat fish," Pa said. Baby Ruth began shaking her head, "No fish! No fish!"

Perla and Pa looked at each other with surprise. Jeffrey laughed but quickly covered his mouth with his hand.

"You like fish," Perla said softly.

Ruth shook her head again saying, "No fish! No fish!"

Pa began passing the food platters around the table. Perla put a small piece of eel on Ruth's plate along with a buttered biscuit. Ruth shook her head, "No fish!" and wouldn't touch her supper.

"Look Ruth," Helen said as she popped a piece of eel in her mouth. "Mmm good."

Ruth looked at Helen and shook her head, "No fish!"

"Ruth it's not fish," Helen said as she took another bite of eel, "It's snake."

Perla looked at Helen sternly. Helen knew she was to say no more.

Ruth looked at her plate and pointed at the eel with a smile, "Snake."

Helen could have crawled under the table. Pa was surely going to give her a whipping after supper. Perla would insist.

Baby Ruth picked up a piece of eel and put it in her mouth. "Ruth eat snake," she said as she began eating her supper.

"Well, I'll be," Pa said as he gave Helen a wink.

After supper Pa sat back in his chair and lit his pipe.

"Pa, I'm going out to paint the smelt tent," announced Jeffrey as he put on his coat.

Helen looked at Pa with pleading eyes. "Can I go help?" Helen asked knowing she should help Perla with the dishes.

Jeffrey stopped at the door and turned to speak to Pa. Pa raised his hand to stop Jeffrey. "Well, Helen I don't know," said Pa as he looked at Perla for her opinion on the matter.

"Seeing as the girl got baby Ruth to eat tonight, I don't see why she can't help paint the tent," Perla said with a smile.

Helen couldn't believe her ears. Perla was actually going to let her do something boyish. Helen slipped on her coat and hurried out the door behind Jeffrey.

In the barn, Jeffrey handed Helen a can of paint and an old brush. "Helen, you paint the door side and try not to slop any paint on the floor or on you," Jeffrey said sternly. "I don't need Perla giving me a tongue lashing."

Helen painted her side of the tent very carefully not getting a drop of paint on the floor or on her dress. When she went around to the side Jeffrey was painting, he had slopped paint over himself and the floor.

"Jeffrey!" Helen said with her hands on her hips, "You have made a mess."

"Don't' worry about it, Helen," Jeffrey said as he put a little more paint on the tent. "Finished!" Jeffrey and Helen stood back and looked at the freshly painted tent.

"Good job, Helen." Jeffrey said as he admired her side of the tent. "Maybe, you can come smelting with me sometime."

Helen looked at Jeffrey with wide eyes and said, "Do you really think Perla would let me?"

Jeffrey put his hand on Helen's shoulder. "You give in to Perla's ways a little and I'll bet she'll give in to yours," Jeffrey said giving Helen a little wink.

* * * * *

Jeffrey's advice worked nicely. Helen started acting more like a young lady – saying please and thank you. She even tried not to speak out of turn or talk with her mouth full. It was hard but when Jeffrey asked Perla if Helen could go smelting with him one Saturday morning. Perla agreed with a smile.

"You see Helen," Jeffrey said as they trudged thru the deep snow to the Bagaduce River. "If you give in a little, you usually get what you want."

"I guess you're right, Perla does seem happier," Helen said as she covered her face with a scarf. Helen had promised Perla that she would try not to wind burn her face. It was hard giving in to Perla's ways. Mama had always let Helen be a tomboy. Mama said there would be plenty of time to be prim and proper when she got older.

Pa and Jeffrey had already hauled the smelt tent onto the river, cut a rectangular hole in the ice, and positioned the tent over it.

"Helen, you wait here while I get some minnows," Jeffrey said as they reached the river's shore. Jeffrey broke the ice at the river's edge and opened the minnow trap. He scooped out a few dozen minnows into a mason jar, then filled it half full with river water.

Helen was excited as they walked out onto the frozen river. You could hear it crack and pop with the movement of the tide. Helen stared at the long cracks in the river. They seemed to go all the way across.

"Stress cracks, Helen, don't worry they freeze right up again," Jeffrey said as he showed Helen that it was cracked open at the top but two inches down the ice was frozen together.

Helen wanted to ask Jeffrey all kinds of questions. The scarf around her face however made talking hard. Her breath had frozen stiff on the scarf.

Once in the smelt tent Jeffrey lit a fire in the metal can wood stove. The stove took very small pieces of wood but they didn't need much fire in such a small enclosure. Helen took off her scarf and mittens and hung them on a line by the wood stove.

Jeffrey broke the ice in the rectangle fishing hole in the floor of the tent. Then started baiting the fishing lines with the live minnows. Putting the hook into their backs so the small fish could still swim. Once baited he weighted the line with a small piece of lead and sunk the line down into the river. Helen baited her share of the lines but she didn't like putting the hook in the minnows back. She couldn't ask Jeffrey for help because he would think she was a sissy.

Helen jigged the lines to entice the smelts while Jeffrey put a few more sticks of wood on the fire.

When the smelts started biting, Helen had a hard time getting hers off the hook. Smelts are small and slippery. Once out of the water they flipped everywhere. Soon Helen just pulled up the lines and Jeffrey would grab the fish and take it off hook. In no time they had caught 36 smelts, enough for a small mess of smelts for supper.

Jeffrey and Pa had caught a croaker sack bag full of smelts every day this week. These smelts had been packed in ice and shipped by mail to Boston or sometimes to New York. When the smelts weren't running very well Pa and Jeffrey would go eeling on the river and these too would be shipped away to either Booth Fisheries in New York or Dench and Hardy in Boston.

When the fire in the small woodstove had finally gone out, Helen and Jeffrey headed home with their days catch.

"Helen, seeing as you helped catch these you can help clean them," Jeffery said flashing Helen a big smile.

"Ladies don't clean fish, Jeffrey," Helen said with her nose in the air. "You just ask Perla."

"We'll see," said Jeffrey as he threw a snowball at Helen hitting her in the shoulder.

Jeffrey and Helen threw snowballs at each other all the way home. When they burst into the house covered with snow, Helen's face red and wind burned.

"Did you have fun, Helen," Perla asked with a smile.

"Yes, I did," Helen answered but when she looked in the mirror she was horrified. "Perla, I'm so sorry I wind burned my face."

"That's ok Helen, we'll put some cream on it later," Perla said as she hung their wraps next to the woodstove to dry. "Let's you and I clean these smelts."

Helen gave Perla a big hug as Jeffrey sat at the kitchen table and watched two young ladies' clean smelts.

Chapter Seven
Ice Harvesting

February and March could be mean winter months in Maine and 1925 was no exception.

"A blizzard is coming," Pa said as he rubbed his back and sat in his favorite chair. "It's going to be a deep snow from the ache in my back."

Just then Jeffrey came into the kitchen stomping his boots in the doorway and brushing the snow from his shoulders. Helen pushed in past him red faced and snow covered, a basket of eggs in her mittened hands. "Some of the eggs are frozen Perla. Do you want me to throw out the ones with the wide cracks?" Helen asked as she walked across the kitchen in her snow-covered boots.

"Put them on the cupboard, Helen and go take your things off in the entryway!" Perla reprimanded. "You're making a mess, leaving puddles everywhere."

"Oh, sorry Perla," Helen said as she hurried back to the entryway dripping more water as she went. "I'll help clean it up I promise."

While Perla and Helen mopped up the puddles on the kitchen floor and tended to the frozen eggs. Pa asked Jeffrey, "Is the barn tight and ready for the blizzard that is coming?"

"Yes, Pa. The animals have all been fed and have extra hay to munch on if we can't get to them early like usual. I strung the blizzard line from the barn to the house, just in case," Jeffrey answered as he warmed his hands over the kitchen woodstove.

"Good," Pa said as he lit his pipe motioning to Jeff to take the seat next to the stove. "Looks like you got chilled to the bone, Jeff, sit and warm up."

"Pa the temperature dropped a lot while I was out in barn. Do you think the animals will be okay?" Jeffrey asked with a worried look at Pa.

"The barn's tight, son they will be fine. We will get water to them as soon as we can in the morning." Pa answered giving Jeffrey an assuring pat on his shoulder.

Just then the two men heard an egg smack on the floor, Perla laugh, and Helen gasp. "It's okay, Helen, it is just an egg," Perla laughed again. "You clean it up and I'll make some popcorn, then we will go in and sit with Pa and Jeffrey."

Pa and Jeffrey looked at each other stunned to hear Perla laugh about a cracked egg on the floor. "Must be the change in the atmosphere, Jeff. I haven't heard Perla laugh since God knows when," Pa whispered to Jeffrey with a smile.

Soon Perla and Helen came into the sitting room with large bowls of popcorn. "This is nice," Pa said when he took his bowl of popcorn. "I feel in the mood to tell a story. Have I ever told any of you about the time Uncle Charlie and I cut ice on Walker Pond?"

Everyone shook their heads no. Jeffrey and Perla pulled their chairs closer to the woodstove and Helen sat on the floor at Pa's feet. They all loved Pa's stories and didn't want to miss a chance to hear one.

Pa sat back in his chair, took a long drink of his coffee, cleared his throat, and begin telling the story. "It was the winter of 1914, just before Helen was born. Jeffrey was almost 6 years old and Perla was 8. Uncle Charlie and I worked for the Maine Lake Ice Company on Walker Pond in Brooksville. It was really cold that winter sort of like this winter but with hardly any snow. A winter without snow brings a cold that goes deep inside your bones. It makes you so cold you could stand on a red-hot woodstove with bare feet and stand there for hours before you began feeling warm.

Uncle Charlie and I dressed in every piece of wool clothing we had and went to work at Walker Pond early in the morning. Your mama and Aunt Samantha packed great lunches with thick meat sandwiches, cookies, some butter, and matches."

"Pa," interrupted Helen. "What were the matches for?"

"Well, Miss Helen," Pa continued. "Uncle Charlie and I used the matches to build a small fire to unthaw the sandwiches and cookies. You see it was so cold that everything in our lunch buckets would be frozen solid by noon time."

"Oh, Pa that sounds awful," gasped Helen. "Why didn't you just stay home and go trapping?"

"We did trap Helen but Uncle Charlie and I wanted to cut ice while it was still being done. About two years later in 1916 the market for natural ice ended and ice was being manufactured by refrigeration. So, there wasn't a need to cut ice any more.

"Pa," Perla asked. "Why did mama and Aunt Samantha pack butter in your lunch buckets?"

"Well Perla that is a good question," Pa answered with a smile. "Sometimes if Charlie and I could get a good fire going we would slather our sandwiches with butter and toast them over the fire. Nothing warms your innards like a nice warm toasted sandwich."

Pa took another long drink of his coffee, "I think I should back up some and give you a little history of the Maine Lake Ice Company. You see a man named George B. Foster of Pittston, Pennsylvania came to Sargentville to visit his sister in the late 1890s. He thought Walker Pond would be a great place to harvest natural ice. George Foster noticed that Walker Pond would be a perfect location to get large quantities of good, clean ice and it was a very short distance from the pond to a deep-water shipping point on Eggemoggin Reach. Mr. Foster also found a ridge between Eggemoggin Reach and the pond to build storage buildings with enough height that would allow gravity to be used some to move the ice blocks. Foster got others to invest in his idea, the plant was built and the Maine Lake Ice Company began operating in 1900 and closed down in 1916."

"The winter of 1914 was really cold with very little snow which meant it would be a good year for ice harvesting. Uncle Charlie and I had always wanted to cut ice. We had done well that year trapping, could afford to cut back our trap lines, and go to work for the Maine Lake Ice Company. The ice was so thick this year that horse and ox teams, as well as people on foot, could cross freely between Deer Isle and the mainland. So off to work we went with our lunch buckets and all the clothing we could get on."

"The ice was just the right thickness, eighteen inches, ripe and ready to be harvested. Now the snow was scraped off and a horse-drawn plough marked grooves on the ice. This was to make a guide for cutting sheets and cakes of ice into the correct dimensions. Now you need to remember that once the ice is cut it is floating in freezing lake water. One wrong move and a fella could slip into that freezing water. As cold as it was that winter, they wouldn't last very long."

Helen gasped, "Oh, Pa be careful."

Jeffrey laughed, "Helen, he was careful. He's right here."

Little Ruth had fallen asleep. Perla picked her up, "Pa can you put the story on hold while I put Ruth to bed?"

"Sure thing, Perla," Pa said as he got up and put a couple more sticks of wood in the woodstove.

Jeffrey looked out the window, "Pa it is really piling up out there. This wouldn't be a good winter to cut ice, would it Pa?"

"No, Jeff, too much snow and last time I measured the ice was only 8 inches thick on the river. Plenty to hold a man while he fishes in his smelt tent," Pa answered.

Perla came back into the sitting room and picked up her crocheting. Pa leaned back in his chair and continued with his story.

"Now the ice is cut and floating in Walker Pond and all us men pole the ice to the loading dock. Then the blocks were placed on a runway and conveyed by a series of endless chains to a storage building. The power for the chains that moved the ice was provided by a large single cylinder steam engine. Other steam engines turned turbines which generated electrical power for the lights and motors throughout the factory."

"On the way up the runway the ice blocks passed under a planner, which shaved them to an equal thickness of about 21 inches. Each finished block weighed about 430 pounds. These blocks of ice were shipped to Baltimore, Maryland and Washington, D.C. by four and five mast schooners. Once in a while a load of ice would even go to the Caribbean and South America."

"To load the schooners with ice there was another runway that ran from the storage buildings to the dock. This allowed ice from storage to be transferred to the deck of the vessel being loaded. All this moving of ice, working on the pond, and just plain walking around to keep the ice moving to storage and to the ships for transport made the ground under foot real icy. Some of the men got the idea to drive some short roofing nails through the bottoms of their boots for traction. They would pound the nail down through their boots from the inside and the pointed end of the nail would be sticking out the bottom. This helped them walk around easier on the icy paths. Uncle Charlie and I liked this idea but didn't want to ruin our boots. So, we opted not to do it and it almost cost me my life."

Helen gasped. Perla stopped crocheting and looked at Pa with astonishment. Pa got up and put some more wood on the fire, then went out to the kitchen to get more coffee. When he came back to the sitting room and sat down in his chair. Jeffrey, Helen, and Perla just looked at Pa waiting for him to continue. Pa took a long drink of his coffee and looked out the window at the swirling snow.

"Pa, please continue," begged Helen.

"Yes, Pa what happened, how did you almost die?" Jeffrey asked with a quiet shaky voice.

"Hay, hay, it wasn't that bad," Pa said matter-of-factly. "Even though your mama thought it was. She wouldn't let me go back to work cutting ice after the accident and Uncle Charlie lost his appetite for ice cutting too," Pa added.

"Accident?" Perla questioned. "How badly were you hurt, Pa?"

"I guess you could call it an accident," Pa said with a smile. "At least that's what your mama called it. To me it was a mishap that could have been prevented. Perla that is how I first hurt my back that now acts up when a storm is coming."

"Please, Pa, tell us what happened?" Jeffrey said as he sat on the edge of his seat.

"Well, Uncle Charlie and I had been working for the Maine Lake Ice Company for near on a month. It was cold every day, hadn't warmed up a smidgin since we started working there. It wasn't like trapping or cutting wood in the winter where the work would warm you up. We stood on the frozen pond, we moved ice in the freezing water with frozen sticks, we pushed and pulled on wet blocks of ice that soaked our woolen mittens freezing them solid chapping our hand red and swollen. You were always cold from the tip of your toes to the ends of your hair."

"Oh, Pa why didn't you just go home?" cried Helen.

"Uncle Charlie and I are not quitters. We were determined to stay and see the job through to the end of the ice season," Pa answered.

"Uncle Charlie and I wondered what on Earth we had been thinking when we signed up to cut ice. But we were there and we had never quit a job before and we didn't want to start then. The day of my mishap had started like any other. It was cold and the wind was blowing. The thermometer on the storage shed said 10 below. However, with the wind blowing it was more like 20 below zero. Charlie and I couldn't get a fire to stay going to warm up our dinner and had to suck on our frozen sandwiches to soften them up enough to eat. We didn't bother with our cookies they were frozen solid as a rock. Without a warm dinner in our bellies, the one thing we looked forward to each day, the cold wind just seemed to suck the life right out of us. Charlie swore his liver froze that day."

Everything was covered with ice, the paths, the runway, the schooner, and the men. We all had beards to keep our faces warm, which did help. Though breathing and talking makes for warm moist air which would freeze solid on your beard and mustache. We all kind of looked like snowmen at least in the face."

"We were all working hard for once the schooner was loaded and, on its way, we could go home to a warm fire and hot meal. John Thurston and Billy Tapley got the runway running from the ice storage shed to the dock and started hoisting blocks onto the track. Well, you know that Uncle Charlie and I had decided not to spike our boots, so walking on the icy path was not easy for us. We were making our way down to the schooner to oversee the loading of the ice when I slipped. My feet went right out from under me and I landed right on my back on the runway track. The fall knocked the wind right out of me, tore my coat hooking me to the track. There was a 430-pound block of ice about five feet in front of me and another one coming down the track behind me."

Perla gasped and Helen shouted, "Oh, Pa!"

Jeffrey shooshed both, nodding to Pa to continue.

"You see the ice blocks are stopped before they are slid in place onto the schooner. And when the front block stopped the block behind me was either going to run over me or squish me to death against the front block." Pa got up from his chair checked the fire and looked out the window at the swirling snow.

"Jeff did you hook the blizzard line to the house when you came in from chores this evening?" Pa asked.

"Hum, ah, yeah Pa I did," Jeffrey answered.

Pa sat back down in his chair and took the last sip of his cold coffee. "Well, you know I was in a predicament. I was hung up tight to the runway track and I was going to be killed by two huge blocks of ice. Well, thank God for Uncle Charlie and his quick thinking. Charlie jumped in the air, landed on his bottom and slid on the ice-covered path to the schooner. Grabbed the crowbar used to keep ice blocks apart and jammed it into the runway track. Charlie's quick thinking stopped the track quick as a wink but gravity was still moving the top block of ice toward me. The back of my coat was so tightly wound into the runway track that I couldn't move my arms to unbutton my coat and my back hurt something fierce. Then all of the sudden John

Thurston and Billy Tapley grabbed me by the front of my coat and ripped me from where I lay. I mean they ripped the back right off my coat to get me free. Within seconds that big 430-pound block of ice slid over my coat back and tunked into the front block of ice."

Perla, Helen, and Jeffrey sat there looking at Pa with their mouths open and their eyes big as saucers.

"Well, I couldn't stand on my feet, I had injured a couple of disks in my back from the fall. They carried me out on a stretcher and took me home to your mama. The doctor came by and told me to stay in bed as long as I could stand it. He had mama put hot compresses on my back and rub it with liniment. Mama made me stay in bed for a week and then I had to use a cane to get around to do the chores for a couple months. My back still bothers me to this day, especially when a storm is coming."

"Uncle Charlie didn't go back to work cutting ice. He helped us out by running both of our trap lines. Kept us going until I could work again. We never got the hankering to cut ice again but we can say we were there when it was done and that is good enough."

"That was quite a story, Pa," Perla said as she put her crocheting in her basket. "So that is how you hurt your back. I remember you being sick in bed when I was 8 but I don't remember how you did it."

"It was a true story, right Pa?" Helen asked with a yawn.

"Yes, it is a true story," Pa said. "I'm not too proud of the fact that Charlie and I would not sacrifice our boots to keep us from getting hurt. It is always better to be safe than sorry. Now off to bed with all of you. I am going to stay up for a while longer to keep the fires burning so the house will be warm when you get up in the morning." With that said Pa went to the kitchen to pour himself another cup of coffee.

Chapter Eight
Ice Hopping

Spring was in the air, but it was still March and if you let your guard down it would set in and snow for a week. Jeffery was outside feeding the animals. Helen had just come in from gathering the eggs. All the hens were now laying again after the older chickens had taken a long winter's vacation.

Perla was just setting a plate of hot biscuits on the table. Everyone had one loaded with butter and a dish of homemade applesauce. Little Ruth made quite a mess with her biscuit, crumbs were all over the floor, it's a wonder she got anything into her stomach.

Jeffery grabbed another biscuit and left the table to finish his chores. Pa had left long before with Uncle Charlie to tend his traps up the Bagaduce River. Helen was in a hurry to finish her breakfast. She knew Jeffrey was going to go up the river to help Pa and she wanted to go.

"Helen, I told you, you can't come," Jeffrey said sternly.

"You're not leaving me here, Jeffrey," Helen said following him close behind.

"Helen I'm going to jump ice cakes up the river," Jeffrey said as he hurried along.

"I can do it Jeffrey, I know I can," Helen said stubbornly.

Jeffrey grabbed Helen's hand. They walked out on the frozen river to where the water was open. The current was floating ice cakes down to the bridge. They were going to jump ice cakes as they floated down the river and make their way up the river. Jeffrey had done this many times with Pa.

"If you must go," said Jeffrey as he grabbed Helen's hand, "You'll have to keep up.

Jeffrey pulled Helen and together they jumped on an ice cake as it floated by. They then ran and jumped onto another.

Helen hadn't realized how hard this was going to be. Her legs were getting tired and her lungs burned. Jeffrey was ahead of Helen. She had to hurry and catch up to him. In her haste she misjudged the distance of the jump. She just missed the ice cake. Helen landed on her chest, her feet going into the icy river water. Helen scrambled up onto the ice cake, hurrying to jump onto the next one. Her wet legs and feet were beginning to go numb.

Jeffrey and Helen reached the shore following the trap line to where Pa was just resetting a trap.

Pa and Uncle Charlie had quite a few hides piled on their sleds. Red fox, weasel, raccoon, Helen was just reaching down to touch one of the pelts when Pa turned and asked, "How'd you get way up here little lady?"

Helen fidgeted for a moment, then stood square shouldered and said, "I jumped ice cakes to get here Pa."

Pa then looked at Jeffrey and Jeff quickly responded, "She wouldn't stay home Pa, it was either bring her or she'd follow anyway."

Pa finished baiting his trap. Checking that the chain was anchored securely. He took his hat off and ran his fingers through his graying hair and sighed, "You can't go back the way you came, Helen."

"Pa, I want to stay and help," Helen said.

"Does Perla know where you are?" inquired Pa.

"No." Helen said as she cuffed the snow with her boot.

"Then, I need to get you home," said Pa.

"Charlie, you and Jeffrey can continue on, I need to take this little lady home," said Pa as he turned to go.

"Sure thing, Sam," said Uncle Charlie as he and Jeffrey grabbed the sled ropes and continued up the trap line.

Helen followed Pa to the rowboat not saying a word. Pa rowed the boat toward home thinking as he rowed about how much he missed his wife. When they reached the path to home Helen was shaking all over.

"Helen are you cold," Pa asked.

Helen began to cry, "Pa, my, my legs are wet."

Pa grabbed Helen up into his arms hurrying up the path to the farmhouse.

Perla met them at the door, "Pa what's wrong."

"Helen has fallen into the river," Pa said.

Pa and Perla quickly got Helen out her coat and wet pants, socks, and boots. Helen's legs were very pale with a blue tinge and very very cold to the touch. Helen was shivering and crying. Perla grabbed a towel to rub Helen's dry.

"Perla, stop!" Pa shouted. "Don't rub her legs you can injure the skin. I'll put Helen to bed. There are some old bricks in the shed put them in the oven to heat up. Warm up some blankets and make some tea. We need to warm Helen up. She's got what they call hypothermia and I think her legs have got frostbite."

Pa carried Helen to her room and gently lie her on the bed. Perla came upstairs with the warmed blankets helping Pa gently wrap Helen in the blankets.

"Perla I'm going for the Doc Hagerty," Pa said as he ran his fingers through his graying hair. "This is all I know to do; I wish your mama was here."

"Me too," said Perla as a tear rolled down her cheek.

"Get that warm tea into her, keep her blankets warm with the heated bricks, and I'll be back as soon as I can with the doctor," Pa reassured Perla as he hurried away to get the doctor. Doc Hagerty lived in Sedgwick Village about ten miles away.

* * * * *

"Perla," Helen murmured. "I'm sorry, Perla. Please forgive me."

"There is nothing to forgive," Perla cooed. "Drink some of this warm tea, sweetheart. We need to get you warmed up."

"Perla, I'm tired," said Helen with a yawn. "My legs feel really tight."

"Stay awake, Helen," Perla quietly pleaded. "Just until the doctor gets here. I'm not sure if I am supposed to let you go to sleep, Helen. Just stay awake."

"I will Perla. I'm cold, can I have another blanket?" Helen asked.

"I have some bricks warming in the oven. I'll get them. Just stay awake," Perla said as she hurried away to the kitchen. In the kitchen Perla took the hot bricks from the oven with a thick pot holder on each hand. She wrapped each brick into a warmed towel and placed them into a heavy wicker basket. Perla carried the heavy basket upstairs. When she entered Helen's room she noticed Helen head was nodding down onto her pillow.

"Helen!" Perla spoke sharply as she gently shook Helen's shoulder. "Helen, you need to stay awake."

"But, Perla I'm so tired. Let me sleep," Helen begged.

"You can sleep after the doctor looks you over," Perla promised. Perla took the cooled bricks from under Helen's blanket, replacing them with the hot towel wrapped bricks. When Perla lifted the blanket, she could see Helen's legs were a bluish purple and the toes on her left foot were reddish and swollen. It took all of Perla's will power not to cringe and looked worried. She continued talking to Helen and pushed the vision of what she had seen from her mind. "After the doctor comes, I'll get you something to eat then you can sleep. But right now, you can have some of this warm tea I sweetened with honey," Perla smiled at Helen clearing her mind of any worry as she fed Helen spoonfuls of the sweet tea. Perla thought it best that Helen didn't worry at least for now about how bad her condition was. Helen was just taking in the last spoonful of sweet tea when Perla heard the door open and men talking in the kitchen. Perla told Helen to stay awake and she would be right back hopefully with the doctor.

Perla calmly entered the kitchen, "Hello Dr. Hagerty.

"Okay Perla, tell me what you know," Dr. Hagerty requested.

"Well, doctor I have had a hard time keeping Helen awake. I have kept her covered with a blanket and have kept warmed towel wrapped bricks around her to make sure she stays warm. Helen has drunk one cup for tea sweetened with honey," Perla reported.

"Have you seen her legs?" Dr. Hagerty questioned.

Perla grimaced and shook her head yes, "It looks bad doctor. Her legs are bluish purple and the toes on her left foot are reddish, swollen, and look shiny."

"I'm going to go see her now and give her a sleeping draft so I can wrap her legs. After she is asleep Perla I will need your help with the wrapping," the doctor told Perla. Then he grabbed his bag and went to Helen's room.

"Pa, Helen's legs look bad, especially the toes on her left foot," Perla said her face white and her brow wrinkled with worry.

"Perla, we need to be strong for Helen. If we are strong, she will find the strength to get through this," Pa said as he kissed Perla on the forehead. "Be strong Perla and stay with Helen. Jeffrey and I will take care of the chores, meals, and housework. Well, maybe I will get your Aunt Samantha to help out some too." Perla hugged Pa tight, he patted her on the back and kissed Perla again on the forehead then left to do the barn chores.

Perla walked into Helen's room a few minutes later. Helen was asleep and Doc was looking at Helen's miscolored legs, studying closely the toes on her left foot. "Perla, I'm going to wrap Helen's legs, they will need to be rewrapped every day. Most likely Helen's legs will blister and I will need to come by every couple days to drain the blisters. In a few weeks the blistered skin will dry, blacken, and peel. New skin will have formed under the blisters. Helen will have some pain, burning, and stinging as she heals. If any of the blisters get infected, I will prescribe a course of antibiotics to treat the infection," Doc instructed.

"What about her toes on her left foot," Perla asked. "They look really bad."

"Yes, they do Perla, but Helen's legs are warm and there is a good pulse in that foot," Doc reassured. "You did a very good job getting her warmed-up Perla. Now do you have an aloe plant?"

"Yes," Perla said as she left the room to retrieve the plant. When Perla returned, she hefted the plant onto the seat of the chair by the window.

"Good, it is a nice big one," Doc said as he cut off one of the large leaves, then split the leaf open on one side with his knife. "Okay, Perla in my bag there are some tongue depressors, get me three or four, then watch how I apply the aloe to Helen's legs." Perla fetched the tongue depressors and watched obediently as Doc smeared aloe on Helen's legs. "Just lightly apply the aloe to Helen's legs. Do not rub the skin and try not to touch the skin with the tongue depressor. After a coating of aloe has been applied wrap her legs loosely but tight enough with gauze bandage so it stays on if Helen moves around in bed. Perla these bandages need to be changed every evening. It is very important that you do this. It may mean the difference between Helen keeping her foot or not. Do you understand Perla?" Dr. Hagerty asked.

"Yes, I understand, doctor," Perla answered as a tear slipped down her cheek.

"Perla, I know this is scary but if you follow my instructions, I am hopeful that Helen will keep her foot," Doc said has he closed his medical bag. "When Helen wakes, she is going to be in pain, give her one aspirin every four hours. If she can't swallow it, crush it up and give it to her mixed with a little sugar and water. If the aspirin doesn't help with the pain, I can give her morphine but I would rather not."

"Doc, is there anything special I should do for Helen's meals and should I bath her?" Perla asked.

"Don't wash her legs, just the rest of her body. Helen can eat what ever you fix her. Make sure she gets plenty to drink, water or warm tea. You need to keep Helen hydrated," Dr. Hagerty answered. "Keep Helen in bed and I will be back in a couple day to check on her."

"Thank you, Doc," Perla said as Dr. Hagerty picked up his bag and left.

Perla brought a chair into Helen's room and sat in it beside the bed. Outside Perla heard Pa drive off in the wagon taking Dr. Hagerty home. Perla put her palm on Helen's forehead, and gave a sigh of relief when it felt cool. She looked over at the supply of gauze bandage and tongue depressors Doc had left for her. Perla wondered if she would have enough aloe plant to help heal Helen. She would have Pa send a message to Aunt Samantha to find a couple more plants so she would have plenty of aloe. All of the sudden Perla felt very tired, exhausted. She wrapped her shawl around herself and fell fast asleep where she sat.

* * * * *

Perla woke later that night to Helen's crying. "Helen, tell me what's wrong," Perla said as she felt Helen's forehead. She sighed with relief still no fever. "Thank you, God!"

"Perla my legs hurt really awful," Helen cried. "Can I take these bandages off?"

"No, Helen leave the bandages on," Perla said while she crushed up an aspirin and mixed it with some sugar and water. "Take this it will help with the pain."

"Perla, that tastes awful," Helen complained.

"Take the rest of it. It will help with the paid," Perla promised. "Now drink this water to wash it down." Helen did what Perla asked without any more complaints.

"Perla, how long am I going to have to be bandaged up?" Helen asked.

"I don't know Helen. Doc said that the bandages need to be changed every evening," Perla responded as she took Helen's hand and lightly squeezing it. "I will do my best to take care of you."

"I know, Perla. I'm tired," Helen yawned. "Your crushed aspirin stuff is working. Thank you, Perla." Helen yawned once again and then drifted off to sleep.

The next week was a frenzy of wrapping and unwrapping Helen's legs, crushing aspirin to keep Helen's pain to a minimum, and aloe plants were

73

everywhere in Helen's room. It seemed that everyone in town had donated their aloe plant to help Helen get well.

Once the town heard of Helen's condition they started cooking, making sure the Gray family had plenty of food to eat. Women took turns coming by to do the dishes, wash the laundry, and sweep the floors. Walter and Moyle came daily to help Jeffrey and Pa care for the animals, then head to their trap lines. Aunt Samantha had taken little Ruth to her home telling Perla, "You focus on getting Helen well and little Ruth can have a vacation at Aunt Sam's house." Perla laughed and cried at the same time as she hugged Aunt Samantha.

By the end of week two Doc said that Helen's legs no longer needed to be wrapped. They had healed well. "Can I get out of bed now?" Helen asked with a big smile.

"Not quite yet," Dr. Hagerty said. "Your left foot doesn't look so good Helen. It is going to be a little longer to get that healed up. Perla told me you are doing quite a lot of crocheting so I brought you some yarn."

"Oh! Thank you, Doc," Helen said as she sat the basket of yarn on her lap to get a closer look at the gift.

"Perla, can you walk me out?" Doc asked as he packed up his medical bag and left the room. Perla followed Dr. Hagerty into the kitchen.

"Perla, you have done a great job nursing Helen. Her legs look great," Doc smiled at Perla and then looked away. "Her left foot isn't doing very well," Doc continued. "Keep it wrapped. Keep Helen in bed and pray, Perla. Here are some antibiotics to give Helen each day, I have written the directions here. I have already talked with your dad; he knows that the foot might have to come off."

"Amputate, Helen's left foot," Perla gasped as she sat hard onto a kitchen chair.

"Perla, I will only take the foot as a last resort. But if the antibiotic doesn't take care of the infection. The foot will have to come off or Helen will die," Dr. Hagerty said as he put a reassuring hand on Perla's shoulder.

Dr. Hagerty left and Perla just sat on the kitchen chair stunned by what she had been told. Perla made her way back to Helen's room. She was going to teach Helen a new crochet stitch but when she entered the room Perla could see that Helen had fallen asleep. Perla sat in the bed side chair and looked at Helen as she slept peacefully.

"Mama, if you can hear me, I need your help," Perla quietly cried out. "Mama, I miss you so, please if you are listening show me how to help Helen." Perla put her face in her hands and cried. After a while, Perla got up poured some water in the basin and washed her face. Perla turned down the lamp and went to the kitchen to make some tea.

When Perla left the room, Helen slowly opened her eyes. In her dream Helen had heard Perla talking to mama but when Helen stirred from sleep, she found that what she thought was a dream was real. Helen listened to Perla cry and realized that Perla missed mama just as much she did. Perla needed mama too.

Perla continued to unwrap, apply aloe, and wrap Helen's foot for the next week. Helen patiently endured having to stay in bed and tried not to fuse at Perla about being bored. Perla no longer had to sit with Helen and little Ruth had come home. Little Ruth sat on the bed and Helen taught her how to play Go Fish and Old Maids.

When Doc Hagerty came the next week, he smiled when he unwrapped Helen's foot.

"You're doing great, Helen," Doc said as he rewrapped Helen's foot. "You will be up and around sooner than I expected." Dr. Hagerty smiled at Helen and gave her a licorice stick and one to little Ruth.

"Thank you, doctor," Helen said quietly.

"Helen, have you used up all the yarn I gave you?" Doc asked.

"Not quite yet," Helen answered. "Perla has taught me some new crochet stitches and I have been practicing those."

"That is great, Helen," Doc said with a smile. "Now maybe you can read this book to little Ruth while I go talk with your sister." Dr. Hagerty handed Helen the book "Doctor Dolittle's Circus" and went to the kitchen to talk with Perla.

Dr. Hagerty sat at the kitchen table and Perla handed him a fresh cup of coffee and a plate of soft molasses cookies. Doc took a big bite of cookie and a drink of his coffee.

"Wow, that hits the spot," Dr. Hagerty said with a smile. "That is one of the best cookies I have eaten in a long time.

"Doc, please!" Perla said with a worried look. "How is she doing?"

"Perla, she is doing great. The left foot is healing well however the toes still have blisters and scabs. A couple still look infected so I want to give Helen another course of antibiotics."

"Another course of antibiotics," Perla frowned. "Is she going to be able to walk without problems?"

"Perla, she is doing great. Helen is healing faster than I expected," Dr. Hagerty reassured. "Actually, I expected to have to amputate Helen's left foot."

"Oh, doctor you mean you're not going to amputate Helen's foot?" Perla cried.

"Perla, that was only going to be a last resort," Dr. Hagerty said as he finished his cookie and took another drink of his coffee. "I want you to keep wrapping the foot and applying the aloe. Helen can go to the kitchen to eat meals with the family but no weight bearing on that foot. She can use crutches but the foot must not touch the floor and must be elevated once she is at the table. Then right back to bed after the meal."

"Really?" Perla smiled with tears in her eyes.

"Yes, really, Perla. Helen will be up and around very soon. Probably with a cane for a while but not for very long," Dr. Hagerty said as he stood up to go. "Perla, can I take some of these cookies home? My wife would love them."

"Yes, of course, doc." Perla smiled as she packed a dozen cookies in a basket. "Thank you so much," she said as she handed Doc the basket of cookies.

"Perla, you did most of the work," Doc said as he went out the door. Perla stood there for a few moments starring at the closed door. Then she hurried to Helen's room to tell her and little Ruth the good news.

Chapter Nine
Alewives and the Peddler

It has been a Few months since Helen's ice hopping accident. Her legs and feet healed well although Helen still walks with a slight limp. Pa, Uncle Charlie, Jeffrey, and Moyle are catching alewives in the brooks and streams that veer off the Bagaduce River to be smoked. Alewife season starts the middle of May and ends around the middle of June. A month of pure fishing joy for the men. This scaly silvery fish comes in from the ocean swims up the Bagaduce river then slip into the brook or steam from which they came as juveniles heading for their home freshwater pond or lake. Once the alewives spawn, they make their way back to the ocean.

It is the alewives that haven't spawned yet that the menfolk want. So, Jeffrey and Moyle set their nets in the mouths of brooks that branch off the Bagaduce River heading to Walker Pond, Parker Pond, and Pierce's Pond early in May. They want to get as many fish that haven't spawned yet. Helen had fussed at Pa to go help set the nets but he gave her a firm, "NO!"

"But Pa!" Helen whined. "I'm healed Pa, I need to get out of the house."

"Absolutely, not!" Pa said as he took hold of Helen's shoulders and looked her in the eyes. "You almost died the last time you ventured out onto the river."

Helen turned away at the sight of the tears in Pa's eyes. "I'm sorry, Pa," Helen whispered. "I'll stay home, I promise."

"Helen, I need you to stay home while Perla is away helping Margaret Flannery birth her baby," Pa said with a smile. "Take care of little Ruth and do some cooking to keep us men going."

"Oh, little Ruth," Helen gasped as she limped hurriedly to the sitting room. "I forgot about little Ruth." When Helen got to the sitting room little Ruth was sound asleep in the middle of the pile of buttons she was stringing.

"She's asleep, Pa, on the floor," Helen said as she reached down to pick up the little girl.

"Here, Helen, let me help," Pa said as he lifted little Ruth into his arms. "I'll put her into her bed, you put some lunch together."

Helen went to the kitchen to make sandwiches for lunch. She pulled a ham from the cool cellar slicing thick slices of ham for the sandwiches. Helen sliced some bread and spread it with butter and homemade mayonnaise, stacked on plenty of thick slices of ham then it topped with another slice of bread spread with butter. Helen cut the sandwiches in half and stacked them on a platter. She then opened a jar of bread and butter pickles and poured the contents into a bowl. Helen made fresh coffee and put a pitcher of cold milk on the table.

"There," Helen said to herself. "That should keep them going until supper." Just then Helen heard Ruth stirring in her room. She limped to little Ruth's room and brought her out to the table to have some lunch.

Jeffrey and Moyle came into the kitchen laughing and joking covered with scales.

"You two need to wash up before sitting at the table," Helen said sternly with her hands on her hips.

"Wow, sis," Jeffrey said as he and Moyle turned to wash up at the kitchen sink. "You sound just like Perla."

"I'm sorry Jeff," Helen whispered as her face turned red. She grabbed the bowl of cookies on the counter and placed them on the table.

"Hey, it's okay, Helen," Jeff replied giving Helen a quick pat on the back. "Moyle and I don't like eating scales with our sandwiches.

"Nice lunch, Helen," Moyle said around a mouthful of sandwich.

Pa and Uncle Charlie came in going right to the sink to wash the scales from their hands.

"This looks good, Helen," Pa said as he sat at the table and put a couple sandwiches on his plate.

Helen poured him and Uncle Charlie a cup of coffee. "Thanks Pa," Helen said she poured coffee for Jeffrey and Moyle.

"Do you have any sugar?" Moyle asked as he grabbed two cookies from the basket. Helen handed Moyle the sugar bowl as she got up to help little Ruth down from her chair handing her a washcloth to wash her face.

"Here Ruth, have a cookie. Now go into the sitting room and pick up the buttons. You still can string buttons but you need to pick up the buttons you scattered all over the floor."

"Yup, I will," said little Ruth around a mouthful of cookie as she hurried into the sitting room.

"Helen, have you had any lunch?" Moyle asked as he looked at Helen's empty plate.

"I'll eat, Moyle when I get a chance," Helen said as she started to clear the table.

"Why don't you sit and have a sandwich," Moyle offered. "Jeff and I will clear the table."

"Moyle, you know we need to hang the brined fish in the smoke house and set this morning's fish to brine," Jeffrey said with a frown. Moyle gave Jeffrey his 'do onto others look' and started clearing the table. "Sit, Helen and eat something while Moyle and I clear the table," Jeffrey added with a half-hearted smile.

Helen sat at the table while Jeff and Moyle cleared the table stacking the dishes by the sink. Moyle filled the kettle on the stove with water to heat for the dishes. "Now Helen, when that water is hot you holler out to me and I will come in to heft it into the sink for you," Moyle said with a smile as he slapped Jeffrey on the back and they headed out the door.

After she finished her sandwich and downed a glass of milk, Helen sat at the table wondering what on earth she would fix for supper. Beef stew. That's what she would make beef stew and hot biscuits. That was something she knew how to make and they all liked it. "When Perla gets back, I'm going to pay more attention to what she cooks and how she cooks it," Helen said to herself in a whisper. The water Moyle had set to heat on the stove was hot so Helen went to the door to holler to Moyle. To her surprise he was standing there reaching for the knob when she opened the door.

"I thought it was about time for the water to be hot," Moyle said matter-of-factly. Moyle hefted the large kettle of water off the stove and poured it into the dishpan in the sink. "There you go, Helen, water for washing and rinsing."

"Thank you, Moyle," Helen said with a smile.

"When you get done with the dishes, why don't you and Ruth come out and help put the brined alewives on the drying sticks," Moyle invited as he left the kitchen.

"We will be right out after the dishes are done," Helen promised. Helen added some cool water and soap to the dish pan, quickly washing and rinsing the lunch dishes. She hefted the Dutch oven (a heavy cast iron pot with a lid) onto the woodstove pushing it to the back of the stove. Then added some lard. When the lard was melted Helen added the beef she had cut into small chunks and coated with a mixture of flour, salt, and pepper. Once she had browned the beef chunks Helen added some water scrapping the brown bits from the bottom of the Dutch oven. She then added chucks of carrot, potato, and onion, added just enough water to cover the vegetables, added a little more salt and pepper giving the mixture a good stir. Helen banked the woodstove to keep it burning for a long time then put the cover on the Dutch oven.

"There," Helen thought with a smile. "If all goes well there will be beef stew for supper." Helen went into the sitting room where little Ruth was stringing buttons.

"Look, Helen," little Ruth said as she held up three long strings of buttons. "I made three necklaces, one for Pa, one for Jeff, and one for you."

"Wow!" Helen smiled. "Ruth you can surprise Pa and Jeff with these tonight after supper."

"That a great idea," little Ruth said as she danced and clapped her hands.

"Let's go outside and help put alewives on drying sticks," Helen told little Ruth as she took her by the hand to get their outside clothing. May in Maine is cool but not cold so Helen made sure Ruth had on a thick wool sweater and boots. Helen knowing that her legs and feet would get cold quickly made sure she put on a pair of thick wool socks and boots. After Helen and Ruth had bundled up for a cool spring day, they headed out to help with the alewives.

The scaly silvery alewives that Jeffrey and Moyle had caught that morning were going to be brined whole because they contained spawn and would make a moister smoked alewife. They had taken the already brined fish out of the barrels, rinsed them with fresh water, put them in buckets next to the smoke house. Jeff and Moyle were rinsing out the brine barrels and filling them with the mornings alewife catch when Helen and Ruth came outside.

Now all Helen had to do was take a drying stick and stick it in the alewife's gill and out its mouth. Pa liked to have about 10 alewives on a stick. Little Ruth didn't like sticking the drying stick into the alewife. So, Helen let her play on the swing while she put the alewives on the drying sticks. Helen stacked the sticked alewives next to the smoke house. Jeff and Moyle could hang the alewives in the smoke house, Helen needed to get inside to check the stew and rest her legs a while before making biscuits for supper.

* * * * *

Helen was just taking a pan of nicely browned biscuits out of the oven when Pa and Jeffrey came in from evening chores. Little Ruth had helped Helen with setting the table. Ruth had sat out plates not bowls for stew and the silverware was not sat in its proper place. "We can practice silverware placement another day," Helen thought to herself as she put the four bowl she had out for the stew on the table. "Ruth, can you sit a bowl on each plate for the stew?"

"Sure!" little Ruth said happily as she did what Helen asked.

"Wow, Helen," Jeffrey said as he sat at the table. "Stew and biscuits, my favorite."

"Helen, those biscuits look really nice," Pa said with a smile taking two and slathering them with butter.

"I helped set the table, Pa," little Ruth beamed.

"The table does look nice, Ruth," Pa said as he picked up his fork to eat his stew. Helen let out a little gasp but Pa winked at her to let her know it was okay.

* * * * *

After the dishes were washed up from supper. Helen helped little Ruth get cleaned up and ready for bed. Pa was going to read Ruth a story in the sitting room while they all shared a bowl of popcorn. Helen planned to go to bed shortly after Ruth was put down. She was tired, it had been a long day, and she couldn't believe it but she missed Perla. Perla made

84

taking care of the house, the cooking, everything looks so easy but it sure wasn't.

"There is stew left over from supper, I can serve for lunch tomorrow," Helen thought to herself. "If Moyle and Uncle Charlie are here tomorrow, I can make some toasted cheese sandwiches to go with it. That will stretch it out to feed everyone. Now what to have for supper?"

"Helen, why are you looking so serious?" Pa asked as he looked up from the story he was reading to little Ruth.

"Just wondering what to have for supper tomorrow night, Pa," Helen answered still wondering what she could put together that would be good but not too hard. Perla knew what foods they had in storage. Helen knew what they had for vegetables as the canned goods, potatoes, and carrots were in the basement. But what did they have for meat?

"Pa, do we have any pork left in the ice house?" Helen asked.

"I think there might be one or two pieces left buried deep under the ice and sawdust," Pa answered. "I'll dig one out tomorrow morning early. Probably will be frozen solid though but should thaw enough by noon to use." Pa added.

"Thanks Pa," Helen said with a big yawn. "I'll make roast pork, boiled potatoes, and carrots tomorrow for supper. And little Ruth and I can make some apple sauce."

"Don't overdo it," Pa warned. "Perla will be back day after tomorrow and just as long as the house is not a total mess, she will be happy. Now go to bed you look like you need some sleep." Pa said as he kissed Helen on top of the head.

Helen headed to bed, dressed in her nightgown, and before her head hit her pillow, she was fast asleep.

* * * * *

Breakfast was easy, oatmeal, fried biscuits, and honey. It was a simple breakfast but Pa had said not to overdo it. Perla's breakfasts were more elaborate but this was filling and would keep Pa and Jeffrey going throughout the morning. Little Ruth had asked to help so Helen let her set the table again making sure Ruth got spoons from the silverware draw for the oatmeal. Pa had brought in the pork roast for supper and it was in the roasting pan thawing on the counter.

"Helen that is the last pork roast in the ice house. There are a couple packages of pork chops and some pork ribs left in the wooden crate under the ice and sawdust. Soon we'll have to get our summer meat from Butcher Frank's wagon when he comes by," Pa told Helen as he spooned honey onto his fried biscuit.

"Pa, I think where it is Saturday tomorrow and Perla is coming home. I'll make baked beans," Helen announced feeling a little embarrassed that she might sound a little like Perla. "Can you get the pork ribs for me? I'm going to put them in the baked beans."

"Are we going to have baked beans or bullets?" Jeffrey asked with a chuckle. "Remember the last time you made baked beans."

"I remember, Jeffrey," Helen said a little red in the face. "I'll soak the beans overnight this time and par boil them in the morning. That should soften them up and the pork ribs will make them real tasty."

"Sounds real nice," Pa said with a smile.

"How about some brown bread too," Jeffrey added with a hopeful smile.

"Jeffrey! That's enough, before you have poor Helen cooking all day. Let's get those ribs for Helen and then tend the fish nets," Pa said as he pushed Jeffrey out the door.

Brown bread. Helen had never made brown bread before. She knew that Perla steamed the brown bread but she hadn't watched how Perla had made it or even how long she had steamed it. Maybe there was a recipe in the recipe box. Helen decided to look for the recipe later. First, she needed to do up the breakfast dishes, then she and Ruth would make some applesauce to go with supper.

Pa came in with the package of pork ribs telling Helen to keep them in the cool cellar. "The ribs won't unthaw very quickly down there and will keep cold until you need them tomorrow," Pa said. "And Helen, the peddler is due to come by in his wagon today. Jeffrey needs a new jack knife and I need some new suspenders. Perla said she wanted some sewing needles and black thread before she left. Here are a couple dollars which should more than pay for everything. Max likes to haggle so tell him right off you will give him a string of smoked alewives for what you are buying. If he doesn't take it, which I'm sure he will. Pay him what he asks and send him on his way."

"Okay, Pa," Helen said rather reluctantly.

"You'll do fine Helen," Pa reassured her. "If you want, we can wait until next week to get the items."

"No, Pa, I can do it," Helen said with more confidence than she felt.

"Good, see you at lunch," Pa said as he went out the door.

"Dealing with the peddler, taking care of little Ruth, keeping house, cooking. Wow! How did Perla keep it all straight?" Helen thought to herself as she retrieved apples from the cool cellar setting them on the table for little Ruth and her to peel.

Soon the apples were peeled, chopped, spiced, and simmering on the back of the stove. The applesauce may be a little sweeter than usual because little Ruth had dumped more sugar in when Helen went to the cupboard to get the cinnamon.

Lunch was another easy meal of heating up leftover beef stew and making a platter of toasted cheese sandwiches. The pork roast was in the oven slow cooking for supper. Helen had rubbed the pork with salt and pepper and placed it in the roaster like she had seen Perla do many times. "I'll keep to easy meals until Perla gets back. She can cook the fancy stuff," Helen thought to herself when she went to the cool cellar to get potatoes and carrots for the evening meal.

When Helen came up from the cellar, she heard the jingle of a horse's harness and a high-pitched whinny coming from the driveway. "Max is here," thought Helen. "Thank goodness little Ruth is taking a nap." Helen put on a heavy wool sweater, grabbed the basket that hung in the cellarway, and went outside to meet the peddler.

Max Abram was a short, olive-skinned, rather stout man who had come to Maine from Syria about five years before. He came around once a week in a fascinating wagon pulled by one beautiful black horse harnessed with a bell ladened harness. Each side of Max's wagon was made up of row after row of drawers that could be pulled out by anyone standing on the ground. These draws contained different kinds of needles, thimbles, thread, ribbons, twine, paper, tacks, jackknives, pencils, and just about anything you could imagine. In the interior of the wagon were shelves which held ready-made clothing and bolts of cloth of many kinds and patterns.

Helen waved to the peddler and Max climbed down from his wagon. The beautiful black horse whinnied and Max fed him a few pieces of grain from his pocket.

"What get you, little girl?" Max asked as he waved his hands toward the wagon.

"I need sewing needles, black thread, a jack knife, and a pair of men's suspenders," Helen told the peddler.

The peddler looked at Helen, "I not understand you words to fast," Max said waving his hands again toward the wagon. Max spoke in broken English with a really heavy accent that made conversation with him very difficult.

Helen realized that to talk with Max Abram she needed to speak very slowly and use her hands to describe the items she wanted. So, Helen pointed to herself and said, "I," then waved her hands toward wagon, "need some sewing needles," Helen said slowly.

"I, yes, sewing needles," Max said clapping his hands together. Helen watched as the peddler went to one of the many draws, opened it, and pulled out a package of sewing needles.

Using the same method Helen asked for the other items she needed. Max put Helen's purchases in the basket Helen had brought out with her. "You pay," Max said as he brought out a pad of paper and pencil figuring out the cost of Helen's purchases.

Helen sat down the basket while the peddler figured on his pad and went to the shed next to the house bringing out the alewives Pa had left for Max. When Max saw the alewives, he put his pad away and his pencil behind his ear.

"You pay, these," Max Abram said with a smile and pointed to the alewives Helen was holding.

"Yes, enough?" Helen asked.

"More," the peddler said with a smile as he went back to his wagon and pulled out a small brown paper bag filling it with penny candies. "This too for you," Max said when he put the bag of candies in Helen's basket. The peddler took the alewives held them to his nose inhaling deeply their salty smoky aroma. Smiling, Max took the alewives from the drying stick and put them in a brown paper bag.

"Even?" Max said with a smile.

"Even," Helen said and picked up the basket waved to the peddler and went back into the house.

* * * * *

Little Ruth helped Helen set the table. Helen showed Ruth how to place the silverware correctly around each plate. The pork roast was on a platter in the middle of the table. Next to it were a bowl of boiled potatoes and a bowl of carrots. A plate of hot biscuits sat next the bowl of applesauce Helen and Ruth had made. Helen had tried to make gravy but it was quite lumpy so she left it on the side board. When Pa and Jeffrey came in from evening chores, they were more than pleased with the pleasant aroma of supper that met them when they opened the door.

"Helen, where's the gravy," Jeffrey said as he heaped his plate with slices of pork roast, potatoes, and carrots.

"Well, Jeff," Helen sighed. "I made some but it didn't turn out very good."

"Helen, it can't be that bad," Jeff said as he scooped his potatoes onto another plate and began to mash them.

"Two plates?" Helen asked with a laugh.

"Yes, Helen. Pork roast dinner requires two plates," Jeffrey said as he slathered butter on his potato and mashed it in. "Where is the gravy, Helen?"

Helen reluctantly went to the side board to retrieve the gravy. "Jeffrey the gravy is lumpy," Helen said as she passed him the gravy.

Jeffrey took a spoon and tasted the gravy, "Helen this gravy tastes just fine," he said and poured gravy over both his plates of food.

"Well, Helen," Pa said with a laugh. "That right there is quite a compliment. When the gravy tastes so good a fella doesn't care about the lumps."

"Jeffrey, do you think you'll have room for the applesauce we made?" little Ruth asked with a look of concern.

"Well, Ruthie if you helped make it, I will make sure I leave some room," Jeffrey promised.

Later that evening Helen sorted, rinsed, and set to soak the dried beans she was going to bake tomorrow for supper. She secretly prayed that this time the baked beans would come out soft and delicious instead of hard and bullet-like. Perla would be coming home tomorrow at suppertime and Helen wanted to surprise her with nice meal.

* * * * *

Helen served the over sweet applesauce leftover from last night's supper for breakfast with fried biscuits. Jeffery praised little Ruth many times during the meal for making such fine applesauce. So much so that Helen finely whispered to him, "Jeff if you keep praising her applesauce, she'll always make it that sweet."

"I really do like the sweetness," Jeffrey whispered back.

Helen cringed and rolled her eyes at Jeffrey, remembering what a big sweet tooth he had.

"Well, Jeff, if you like sweets so much why don't you put some of the penny candy Max Abram gave me yesterday in your pocket before you leave," Helen said as she pointed to the cupboard over the sink.

"I think I will," Jeffrey said as he pulled the penny candy from the cupboard and put a fistful in his coat pocket. "Thanks Helen."

Now that Pa and Jeffrey had left the kitchen to work outside and little Ruth was amusing herself by attempting to wash the dishes. Helen set to getting the beans in to bake.

The dry beans Helen had set to soak the night before had swelled up nicely. So, Helen dumped out the remains of the old water and covered the beans with fresh water, parboiling them until the bean skins had split. She had soaked way more beans than she needed, so she would need to make two pots of beans. Helen went down cellar and retrieved two pieces of salt pork from the brine crock making sure to cover it tight. She also grabbed a jug of molasses to sweeten the beans. With a piece of salt pork in each pot Helen poured in some of the beans. She then put in the pork ribs Pa had got for her from the ice house that she had rubbed with salt and pepper, then poured in the reminder of the parboiled beans. Helen mixed molasses, dry mustard, salt, pepper, and hot water together, pouring the mixture into each bean pot. Once the beans were in to bake and the fire was banked. Helen gave a sigh of relief, "There, maybe this time the baked beans will come out okay."

"They will be good," little Ruth said as she wiped her soapy water dripping hands across the front of her dress.

"I hope so, Ruth," Helen laughed. "I think we better get you into a dry dress. Then you can play with your dolls for a while."

While little Ruth played with her dolls, Helen put her feet up and read over the brown bread recipe she had found in the recipe box. She was going to attempt brown bread but Helen was going to make yeast rolls too just in case the brown bread was a flop. As Helen read through the recipe, she thought to herself, "The batter doesn't look too hard but you have to steam the bread in a can." Helen went to the kitchen and looked through the cupboard for a can that Perla would have used to make the brown bread. She found a couple cans that looked right and set them on the sideboard. Pa came in from outside stamping his feet of dirt before he entered the kitchen.

"Helen, Jeff and I are going out on the river to check the alewife nets," Pa said as he grabbed a couple cookies from the cookie jar. "We won't be here for lunch."

"Do you want me to put a couple sandwiches together?" Helen offered. "We have some pork roast leftover from supper."

"That sounds fine, Helen, if you have time," Pa said as he looked at the brown bread cans on the counter.

"I have time, Pa," Helen said reassuringly. Helen sliced the bread for the sandwiches as Pa retrieved the cooked pork roast from the cool cellar. She spread butter and mustard on the bread and topped it with thick slices of pork roast, cut the sandwiches in half wrapping them with waxed paper. Helen placed the sandwiches in a paper sack along with the remainder of the cookies from the cookie jar.

"Thanks, Helen," Pa said as he headed out the door. "Those beans smell really good."

Helen cleaned up from the sandwich making. Then set to the task of making the brown bread. She made the batter, then greased the steaming cans, filling the cans half full with batter as instructed by the recipe. Helen put the canner on the stove putting the jar rack upside down on the bottom. This was to keep the cans of brown bread from being directly on the bottom of the canner. She added about three inches of hot water to the canner, set the batter filled cans on the jar rack, and put the cover on the canner.

"There, Helen," said to herself. "In thirty minutes hopefully, we will have brown bread to go with the baked beans." Helen opened the oven door and stirred the baked beans, poured in a little more water and molasses.

"Mmm, that smells good," little Ruth said when she came into the kitchen. "Helen, I'm hungry."

"Okay, Ruth, I'll make you a sandwich," Helen offered as she put a couple sticks of wood into the cook stove.

Ruth and Helen each had a roast pork sandwich and a little applesauce. "Ruth, do you want to help me make some yeast rolls?" Helen asked while she cleared their lunch dishes.

"Yes! Yes!" Ruth shouted clapping her hands.

After washing their hands really well. Helen showed Ruth how to measure the ingredients. Then together they kneaded the dough. When the dough was set to rise, Helen cleaned the flour from Ruth's hands, face and dress.

"Okay, Ruth," Helen said. "You clean up all your dolls in the sitting room. Then I'll let you help me set the table and form the rolls."

"Yes," said Ruth as she hurried to the sitting room to take her dolls back to her room.

Helen took the baked beans from the oven. They smelled good and looked good. Helen took a small saucer from the cupboard and spooned a few baked beans into it to cool. When she tasted the beans, she closed her eyes and let out a sigh of relief. Her baked beans tasted really delicious. Helen then took the brown bread from the canner and placed it on the side board to cool. "It looks like brown bread," she said to herself. "And smell really good. Well, I need to wait for it to cool before I take it out of the cans."

"Come here Ruth," Helen called out. "Let's shape these rolls, so we can set them to rise again."

"Coming," Ruth called back running into the kitchen to the sink to wash her hands.

"Wow! Ruth, you remembered to wash your hands," Helen praised. Helen let Ruth punch down the dough. She then cut the dough into 24 equal pieces letting Ruth shape half the dough into rolls. When they finished Helen covered the pan with a cloth and set the rolls to rise. The rolls definitely were not identical but Helen was sure they would be delicious. They were made with love.

Ruth and Helen set the table adding a dish of bread and butter pickles along with a dish of green tomato pickles. "Looks good," little Ruth said with her hands on her hips.

"Yes, it does," Helen agreed. "Let's check the rolls to see if they are ready to go in the oven. Perla will be here in less than an hour."

The rolls had risen nicely so Helen put them in the oven. "Don't let me forget the rolls," Helen said to Ruth with a smile. "Let's wash your face and hands Perla will be here soon."

Helen was taking the brown bread out of its cans when Pa and Jeffrey came into the kitchen. "Jeff, can you taste this to see if it is fit to eat," Helen said as she passed Jeffrey a small piece of brown bread.

Jeffrey smelled the piece of brown bread that Helen passed him, then slowly tasted the bread with his tongue. Still slower Jeff took a small bite. Then he popped the whole piece in his mouth. "Doesn't taste like poison," Jeff said with a laugh. Helen put her hands on her hips and stamped her foot. "Helen, your brown bread tastes great," Jeffrey said reassuringly. "It would be even better with those great smelling beans on top." Helen smiled, continuing to slice the brown bread and placing it on a platter.

"Helen," Ruth said as she pulled on Helen's skirt. "The rolls smell done!"

"They do," Helen replied opening the oven to check the rolls. "Well, they sure look done too, Ruth." Helen took the rolls out of the oven, brushed them with melted butter, then placed them in a basket covered with a cloth putting them on the table.

A jingling of a horse's harness let them all know that Perla was home. Little Ruth began to dance around the kitchen until Pa picked her up to go out and greet Perla. In the driveway stood a beautiful chestnut colored horse attached to a small wagon. Helping Perla out of the wagon was Mr. Baxter the Baptist minister. Perla was all smiles and happier than Helen had ever seen her. Little Ruth ran to Perla and Perla gathered her up in warm hug.

"I missed you Perla," little Ruth said as she hugged Perla tight. "Helen and I have been cooking and I helped make supper."

Perla looked at Pa with a smile. "Perla, Helen has done a great job taking care of all of us," Pa reassured Perla. "And Ruth here has been a great help too." Pa turned to Mr. Baxter, "Would you like to stay for supper, minister?"

"Say yes," little Ruth chimed in. "Helen has made baked beans and brown bread. And I helped make yeast roll and helped set the table."

"It sounds great," Mr. Baxter said with a smile grabbing Perla's travel bag. Perla blushed a little pink and Helen ran into the house to set a place for the minister.

Chapter Ten
Blueberries

By July Helen's limp was completely gone and she was doing as much of the cooking as Perla. This allowed Perla time to go out on dates with Jon Baxter the Baptist minister. Helen knew that Perla felt that she and the young minister could only be friends and that was as far as it could go. But each time Perla came home from a date with Jon she was happier than Helen had ever seen her. Helen was hoping that Perla would get serious about Jon Baxter and eventually marry him someday.

Then came the news that Jon Baxter was leaving and wasn't sure when he would be coming back to Sedgwick, if ever. He had been called away to a parish in Aroostook county and wasn't sure how long he would be there. Perla didn't even cry. She kept going like nothing had happened. The next week the whole family would be in the blueberry field and Perla insisted that the house be cleaned from top to bottom. She put dust caps on each of girl's heads, had Helen and Ruth wear their oldest dresses, then they cleaned the house like it had never been cleaned before. When Pa asked why the house needed to be so thoroughly cleaned. Perla answered, "We will all be in the blueberry fields soon and will be too tired to do any cleaning when we are home." Pa just smiled and looked into Perla's eyes for the true answer. Perla looked happy but as he looked into her eyes, he could see a great sadness there.

* * * * *

Near the end of July came the time of year Perla disliked the most, blueberry season. Pa and Jeffrey took a field to rake every summer. This summer the field they would be raking was on the Sedgwick Ridge. Uncle Charlie, Moyle, and Walter were hired on to help rake. The berries the menfolk raked were sold to the Allen's Factory in North Sedgwick where the blueberries were canned. Wearing big floppy hats to protect their faces from the sun, Perla, little Ruth and Helen picked berries in quart boxes which were crated fresh and shipped to Boston.

Perla and Helen could pick berries really clean and fast. Little Ruth's berries were full of leaves, were squished into the quart box, and Ruth's face and hands were blue with berry juice. Perla wiped little Ruth's face and hands removing what she could of the blueberry juice. Then she had Ruth get a new quart box and showed Ruth how to carefully remove the berries from their stems. Only pulling off the berries not the leaves. "You need to pick slower and more carefully," Perla instructed. "If you pick this box of berries cleaner and don't squish them you will earn some penny candy the next time the peddler comes to the house."

"Oh, Perla!" Ruth gasped. "Yes, I would really like some candy." Ruth sat on a rock and carefully picked blueberries putting them into her box. It took her quite a while but when Ruth was finished, she had picked a quart of really nice-looking blueberries.

"Here you go, Perla," Ruth said as she wiped her blueberry-stained hands across the front of the apron Perla had insisted she wear over her dress.

"Good job! Ruth," Perla said with admiration. "Here, now you can pick another box."

"No thank-you, Perla," little Ruth said. "I'm tired. I'm going to go sit under that tree over there." And little Ruth walked away and sit under a big oak in its shade.

"Okay, Ruth, you stay right there," Perla demanded.

"I will," Ruth replied as she leaned up against the tree's trunk. Soon little Ruth was fast asleep in the shade of the old oak tree.

Perla and Helen continued picking berries until lunch time. By then it was too hot to pick or rake berries in the field. At noon Pa, Jeffrey, Uncle Charlie, Moyle, and Walter along with Perla, Helen, and a sleeping Ruth got into the back of the wagon and headed home for lunch. Everyone would come back in the evening to pick and rake when it was cooler.

Before anyone could have lunch Perla demanded they wash as much of the blueberry stain from their hands as possible. She also made Pa and Jeffrey change their clothes if they wanted to sit in the sitting room. Today's lunch would be ham sandwiches, cold milk, and cookies.

"Pa, it's too hot to lite the stove for coffee," Perla said. "I do have some cold tea, if you'd like some?"

"Do you have any coffee left from morning?" Pa asked. "I'll have that cold with some milk and sugar." Perla poured Pa a cup of cold coffee and handed him the sugar bowl. The jingling of a horse's harness sounded from the driveway.

"Who could that be?" Perla said as she looked out the kitchen window. "It's Jay Douglass the mail driver. We rarely get mail." Perla said as she went out to greet the mail driver.

Jay Douglas was the Rural Free Delivery, RFD for short, mail diver for Sedgwick. He drove summer, winter, rain, shine, or snow. Jay Douglas drove a one-horse wagon in good weather and a sleigh in the winter. The mail which consisted mostly of letters and postcards were kept in a large leather pouch beside him on the seat. Also on the seat beside him was a small tin box with a hinged cover where he kept stamps and cash.

"Hello, Mr. Douglas," Perla said with a big smile. "What do you have for us?"

"Well, Perla, I have a letter for you," Mr. Douglas said as he handed Perla the letter.

"For me?" Perla asked with surprise as she took the letter. Perla read the return address and gasped, "It's from Jon Baxter."

"Thank you, Mr. Douglas," Perla said as she put the letter into her apron pocket.

"You're welcome," Mr. Douglas said as he turned his wagon around and headed down the road to continue his mail route.

Perla went into the house smiling broadly and started to clear the lunch dishes from the table.

"Are you going to finish your lunch, Perla?" Pa asked. "And what did the mail driver want?"

"No, Pa, I'm not hungry," Perla answer. "He had a letter from a friend for me. If you don't mind, I would like to go read it now." Perla said as she left the kitchen in a hurry heading toward her room.

"Pa!" Helen began to complain. But Pa raised his hand to stop her and Helen fell silent. Helen finished clearing the lunch dishes and quickly washed them. She was dying to know what was in Perla's letter but knew best not to pry.

* * * * *

Perla was happier than usual during blueberry season. However, she was stricter than ever with making Helen and Ruth wear big floppy hats while in the field and with the nightly hand scouring with lye soap to remove the blueberry stains.

"Blueberry-stained fingers and sun freckled faces are not very becoming for young ladies," Perla said each evening when she made Ruth and Helen scrub their hands.

One night when Helen was really tired of both picking blueberries and listening to Perla's nightly chant said, "Perla I don't think hands scrubbed raw with lye soap are very becoming for young ladies either!" With that Helen stomped to her room refusing to scrub the blue from her fingers.

"Helen Elizabeth Gray, you come back here!" Perla demanded. "That blueberry stain needs to be washed from your hands before you go to bed."

"Perla, leave her be," Pa admonished.

"But Pa, her sheets will get blueberry stained," Perla contested.

"Perla, she washed her hands before supper," Pa said calmly. "Any juice that would stain her sheets was washed away then, let it be."

"But Pa her hands…," Perla started to complain and Pa stopped her in mid-sentence.

"Let it go, Perla," Pa said as he went to check on Helen. When he opened the door to her room, he could see that Helen had fallen asleep on her bed fully clothed. He covered her with a light blanket and quietly closed the door. When he went back to the sitting room Perla was ushering little Ruth off to bed.

"Perla, let Helen be, she is asleep," Pa commanded. "She needs her rest." Pa knew if he had told Perla that Helen had fallen asleep fully dressed. Perla would have wanted her to be awoken to undress for bed. Pa had spoken and Perla would respect that.

* * * * *

About a week later something glorious happened that threw Perla's real lady theory out the window. It was going to be a really hot August day in 1925. The August flies were buzzing and it was only seven o'clock in the morning. There were dew webs all over the grass which Moyle said meant there was a storm coming.

"We're probably going to get a humdinger of a thunder storm tonight," Moyle mused as he seated himself in Pa's wagon.

"It's going to be a hot one," Pa said as he helped little Ruth into the back of the wagon. "Perla, Helen, do we have plenty of water?"

"Yes, Pa, there's plenty," Perla replied. "Girls, put your hats on."

"Perla, can't we wait until we get in the field?" Helen retorted.

"Perla, I don't know why you make these girls wear hats while they're picking berries," Moyle said with a frown. "Hats make you extra hot in this kind of weather."

"The sun will brown their faces and give them freckles," Perla snapped. "Sun freckled faces are not very becoming for young ladies."

"I like young ladies with freckles," Moyle replied with a smile giving Helen a wink.

"Me too," chimed in Jeffrey and Walter together.

"Oh, you can keep your hats off until we get to the field. But when we get there, I want them on your heads," Perla ordered.

Helen smiled at Moyle to quietly thank him. To cushion her bottom on the bumpy ride to the field Little Ruth sat on her hat. Perla climbed into the back of the wagon, sat down with a humph, crossed her arms in front of her looking cross and disgusted with all of them. Moyle laughed which made Perla even madder.

When they reached the field, they were raking on Sedgwick Ridge a buggy was parked with a woman standing next to it. "That must be Miss Blodgett," Pa said as he steered the wagon toward a stand of trees, parking it in the shade. As Pa helped Perla out of the wagon he told her, "I saw Miss Blodget at Frank

Gray's store the other day and she asked if she could pick blueberries with us. She wants to earn a little extra money. I couldn't see a problem sharing the wealth of the field with somebody who wanted to work." Perla just shook her head in response.

"Boys, take Miss Blodgett's horse and buggy over in the shade for her," Pa said as he and Uncle Charlie grabbed the rakes and buckets from the wagon.

"Sure thing!" the three boys chorused together as they hurried to do what Pa had asked.

"Perla, can you show Miss Blodgett where you girls are picking berries and give her some boxes?" Pa asked as he, Uncle Charlie, and the boys set to work raking blueberries.

"Hello, Miss Blodgett. I'm Perla," Perla said with a smile handing the young woman some quart boxes to pick in. "We are picking berries over here," Perla directed. "Girls put on your hats!"

"Oh, please call me Hattie," Miss Blodgett said with a big smile which showed a lite blue stain on her teeth and lips. Miss Hattie Blodget had been eating blueberries and stained her teeth. Helen thought Perla's chin would drop clear to the ground. Perla would never eat blueberries because they stain your teeth and proper ladies didn't go around with blue teeth.

"Um, Hattie, have you every picked blueberries before?" Perla asked, trying not to stare at Hattie's blue teeth.

"Why yes, Perla. I'm from Cherryfield and usually go home each summer to pick in my dad's fields. But dad has plenty of help this summer and I decided to stay in Sedgwick," Hattie answered with a lite blue smile.

It was true, Miss Hattie Blodgett could sure pick blueberries. She picked as many as Helen and Perla put together. By eleven o'clock it was so hot Helen could feel a river of sweat trickling down her back. The rim of the hideous hat that Perla made her wear was soaked with sweat and stuck to her head. Pa decided that they would break for lunch an hour early. They would come back in the evening and hopefully it would be cooler. Miss Hattie told Pa she would be back in the evening too and left in her buggy waving a blueberry-stained hand.

"Pa, I can't believe the local teacher would be out picking blueberries and eating them making her teeth blue. She doesn't even wear a hat to keep her face from browning," Perla said with disgust. "She is not setting a very good example for the children."

"Perla, she is a hard worker and that is the best example to be setting," Pa said sternly.

Lunch was very quiet they were all tired from working in the hot blueberry field. Little Ruth fell asleep in her chair and Pa took her to her room to put her down for a nap. Pa dozed in his chair in the sitting room while Perla sat working with her crochet cotton making a doily. Helen went to her room to rest and Jeffrey took a nap in the shade of the big oak in the yard. That evening the blueberry crew met back in the field. They were only able to work for a couple hours before an ominous black cloud started across the sky grumbling thunder in the distance. As Moyle had predicted that morning there was a humdinger of a thunder storm that night.

The next morning Miss Hattie Blodgett was waiting for them this time with her buggy parked in the shade. Helen could see Hattie wore the same blueberry-stained apron from the day before and her hands were still stained blue. Miss Blodget hadn't scrubbed her hands the night before to remove the blueberry stain.

"Hello Perla, Helen, Ruth," Miss Hattie said pleasantly. "What a fine thunder storm we had last night. It cleared the air nicely."

"Yes, yes it did," Perla shuddered unable to take her eyes off Hattie's blueberry-stained hands. "Pardon me Hattie, do you need some lye soap to get the blueberry stain from your hands?"

"Oh, no thanks, Perla. I don't bother to scrub my hands until after blueberry season is over. I do wash my hands to get the sticky and dirt off, I don't mind the blue stain," Hattie answered matter-of-factly as she picked up a quart box making her way to the field to pick berries.

"Miss Hattie doesn't care about having blue stained hands, she doesn't wear a hat, and she has a fine mask of freckles across her nose," Helen thought to herself.

"Let's get to work," Perla said as she grabbed a quart box. Then whispering to Helen, Perla said, "Put your hat on. No one will ever ask you to marry if you look like Miss Hattie."

The thunder storm had cooled the air considerable. It was still a hot August day but there was a slight breeze that added some relief. The crew that now included Miss Hattie decided to work until one o'clock today and not come back this Friday evening to work.

"What do you think about having a cookout Saturday," Pa asked. "We can cook on the fire pit." Pa and Jeffrey had made a fire pit for Perla and Helen to roast meat on so they didn't have to heat the house up with the wood stove during the summer months.

"Sounds good," Moyle said. "I'll bring a couple rabbits."

"You sure you can get a couple rabbits, Moyle?" Walter laughed.

"At least a couple," Moyle retorted folding his arms across his chest.

"If I'm invited," Hattie said. "I will bring a blueberry pie."

"Of course, you're invited," Pa laughed. "You're part of the crew."

Everyone worked hard the rest of the afternoon and finished the field they had been working. They would have this weekend off and would be moving to another field on the other side of the ridge on Monday.

* * * * *

The Saturday afternoon cookout was a great relaxing time. Moyle brought three rabbits all skinned and ready for roasting. Aunt Samantha came she had been working at Allen's Blueberry factory picking over blueberries to be canned. Perla was shocked to see that Aunt Samantha's hands were as blueberry stained as Miss Hattie's. When Miss Hattie Blodgett's buggy drove up the driveway there were two people seated inside. A tall handsome man jumped out the driver's side of the buggy and Perla gasped. It was Jimmy

Sargent. He helped Miss Hattie from the buggy blueberry-stained hands and all.

"I hope you don't mind, Perla. I brought Jimmy my fiancé," Hattie said as she handed Perla a fresh blueberry pie.

"The more the merrier," Perla said politely. "I'll put this pie on the table. It will go great with the ice cream Helen and Ruth are churning."

"Oh, do save me some ice cream," Miss Hattie said with a smile. "I love ice cream with blueberry pie."

"Who's that Perla with Miss Hattie?" Helen asked as she put more salt on the ice in the ice cream freezer.

"It is Jimmy Sargent, Miss Hattie's fiancé," Perla said with astonishment.

"It looks like, Miss Hattie has done pretty good for herself. With her blue teeth and blueberry-stained hands," Helen laughed.

"Stop it, Helen. That's rude," Perla said with a huff. "Make sure you don't churn that ice cream into butter. Perla couldn't believe how Miss Hattie had found such a fine man when she didn't even try to look like a proper lady. Perla looked over at Hattie with her fiancé Jimmy. Hattie was dressed nicely; Jimmy was holding her blueberry stained hand. He didn't seem to care that she had freckles across her nose or blueberry stains on her fingers. Jimmy only cared for her. Perla remembered what Moyle had said, "I like young ladies with freckles." Maybe Perla had been wrong, maybe being a lady was more than pretty hands and a flawless face.

"Perla," Miss Hattie said startling Perla out of her thoughts. "Your pa tells me you went to school to be a teacher."

"Yes, I went to Eastern State Normal School in Castine but I didn't finish," Perla said a little embarrassed.

"Oh, I know Perla you came home when your mama died," Hattie said, not with a look of pity but with a look of understanding. "I need a favor; Perla and I think you are the one to help me. You see Jimmy and I are getting married this fall and I need a good substitute teacher for two weeks. Your pa said he could spare you for that time. What do you think?"

"A substitute teacher, me?" Perla asked stunned. All she every wanted was to be a teacher.

"Think about it Perla and give me your answer in a couple days," Hattie said beaming with anticipation. "I know you would make a great teacher. Hattie grasped Perla's hands with her blueberry-stained hands giving them a little squeeze. Perla smiled brightly back at Hattie. She couldn't believe the opportunity she had just been offered.

"I'll talk to Pa and Helen, and give you my answer Monday," Perla said giving Hattie a lite hug before Jimmy coaxed her into getting a piece of blueberry pie and fresh churned ice cream.

* * * * *

The next Monday when they were getting ready to go to the next field to rake Helen and little Ruth could not find their hats. "Perla will be mad if we don't find our hat," little Ruth said as she gave Helen a worried look.

"Come on girls, let's go," Perla called from the kitchen.

Ruth and Helen went to the kitchen expecting Perla to be angry because they didn't have their hats. "Go get in the wagon, girls," Perla said with a smile. "We're ready Pa."

"Perla, we can't find our hats," Helen confessed looking worried.

"We don't need them today," Perla answered. "Hats make you too hot."

Ruth and Helen looked at each other than turned and hurried from the kitchen to the wagon.

Moyle picked up little Ruth and swung her into the wagon, "Where are your floppy hats girls?" he asked as he gave Helen a hand up into the wagon.

"We don't know," Helen replied. "Perla said we don't need them Moyle. I think something has happened to Perla."

"Oh, Helen I don't think anything bad has happened to Perla," Moyle reassured her. "Perla is just realizing that her way may not always be the right way."

Chapter Eleven
Coming Full Circle

Helen looked in the mirror at her sun-tanned face and fine mask of freckles across her nose. She liked what she saw. Blueberry season had become more fun once Perla stopped making them wear big floppy hats and scrub their hands each night with lye soap. Helen was a year older now. The last year had been so different without Mama. It had been sad, happy, lonely, frightening, confusing, not normal but what was normal anyway. Normal was having Mama there to confide in, help her, Jeffrey, Perla, and little Ruth grow into strong, independent adults but Mama wasn't here any longer. She had been there for Jeffrey, Perla, and even Helen and had helped them get on the right path toward adulthood. Little Ruth would probably not remember Mama at all. Helen would help little Ruth, teach her all the things Mama had taught her and Perla would too.

After breakfast had been cleared from the table and the dishes done Perla and Helen were going to Mama's grave at Camp Stream Cemetery. Little Ruth had stayed at Aunt Samantha's the night before to get a little spoiling and so Perla and Helen could have some private time at Mama's grave.

"It's been a year Mama, since you left," Perla said as she put the flowers she brought on Mama's grave.

"We've done pretty well, Mama," Helen added as she put her flowers down on the grave. "Perla and I have even learned to work together. Helen looked over at Perla and saw Perla wiping away tears from her cheeks. Helen reached over to hold Perla's hand. The two girls stood there in silence holding hands reading the words etched into Mama's grave stone.

Addy Louise Gray
11/24/1818 – 8/17/1924
died in childbirth
~ Forever in your heart ~

"Perla, my heart still hurts, I miss her so," Helen cried freely letting the tears roll down her cheeks.

"I know, Helen, I know," Perla said as a large glistening tear fell from her cheek and splashed on the petal of the fall rose that was planted on Mama's grave.

"Pa must have planted this rose bush," Perla said. "He knew how much Mama loved roses, especially fall roses."

Perla and Helen fall silent again for a while. Wondering about Pa and how many times he had come to Mama's grave over the past year. Pa seemed to be coping well but was he really? He never showed his sorrow. Pa had been a rock for all of them.

"Perla will you every marry?" Helen asked.

"No, by the time little Ruth is out of school I will be too old to marry," Perla answered.

It seemed unfair to Helen that Perla had to give up her life to take care of them.

“Perla, are you going to substitute teach for Miss Hattie?” Helen asked, hoping this will spark the interest in teaching in Perla again.

“Yes, I’m going to substitute for Miss Hattie in October,” Perla said with a little smile. The smile told Helen that Perla was still interested in being a teacher. “Miss Hattie said if it worked out well, I could be her substitute teacher when she needed to be away. That will have to be enough, Helen. I can’t be a full-time teacher. Helen this is what I am supposed to do, raise you and little Ruth,” explains Perla. “This is the kind of teacher God intended me to be. I will help you and Ruth become strong young women.”

“Perla, you don’t have to do it alone,” Helen told her. “I plan to help raise little Ruth too. You don’t have to give up your dreams Perla.”

Perla looked at Helen remembering how she had helped when Perla was away helping with the birthing of Margaret Flannery’s baby. Helen had cooked and taken care of little Ruth by herself.

“I believe Helen you are more than capable of helping raise little Ruth,” Perla said with a smile. “Miss Hattie said if I did a good job substituting, she would write a letter of reference to the dean of teachers at Eastern State Normal School. My substituting may be enough to complete my training for a teaching degree.”

“You want to be a teacher and I want to be a farmer. We can help each other accomplish our dreams,” Helen said with a smile.

Helen and Perla walked away from Mama’s grave toward home. The girls had become more than sisters, they had become friends. As they walked down the path toward home, they saw a beautiful chestnut colored horse attached to a small wagon in the yard. Jon Baxter standing next to the wagon with a bouquet of flowers waiting for Perla.

Helen thought to herself, "It's funny how you think life is going to be one way. Even make plans for it to be that way. Then everything changes in an instant and life directs you onto a totally different path. It looks like Perla may get married, eventually and might even get to be a teacher, someday."

With that Helen walked into the house to get supper started.

It's not really the end, just another new beginning…

About the Author

Susan Varnum was born and raised in Maine and now resides in Harborside, Maine with her husband, grandson, dog, cat, and chickens. She is a special education teacher who loves to write. Susan uses this talent to encourage her students to write their own creative stories about what interests them. *More Than Sisters* is Susan's first children's book, which her 7th and 8th grade students read and encouraged her to publish.